The Badge
and the Bride

Badge and the Bible Series

Terry W. Burns

LONE MESA PUBLISHING

The Badge and the Bible

PROLOGUE

Buck Green was a small-town sheriff who pastored a church on the side… Or was he a small-church pastor who also wore a law enforcement badge? It was a question Buck struggled to answer. Walking the line between the badge and the Bible could be difficult and involved many choices and much soul-searching, but many questions still remained.

DEDICATION

Dedicated to Teri Burns, publisher, editor, cover designer, sounding board, advisor, and the best daughter a man could have.

CHAPTER 1

"Clem, do you see what I see? Is that a leg sticking out from under that bush?" The two men moved on unsteady legs down the dusty dirt road.

"You're being silly, Billy Bob, bushes don't have legs."

"I mean somebody's leg sticking out, you moron."

"Who you calling a moron? You're the one seeing bushes with legs on 'em."

It was after 10 p.m.; there was no moon, and they strained to see. Billy Bob gave a deep sigh. A thick cover of mesquite bushes bordered the road tight on both sides. "I guess Sam was right to take our pickup keys away from us because I really think I see some *person's* leg sticking out over there."

Clem rubbed his eyes before he leaned over and tried to focus. "Well I'll be switched, I see it now. Who do you suppose it is?" He rubbed his forehead as if it would help him remember. "Who left the bar before we did? Wasn't it Wilbur?"

Billy Bob snickered. "Yeah, he was really hammered."

"Like we ain't? We oughta see if we can get him up out of there."

"You got that new-fangled phone on you? Let's take his picture with it. We can have some fun with that after he sobers up."

Clem started shooting video while his friend moved into the brush. Billy Bob went down on one knee. "Man, this ain't

Wilbur…and this dude is dead."

Clem moved in closer to film the body. "You recognize him?"

Both men sobered up significantly. "I can't tell just from the light of that phone. Besides, his head is pretty messed up."

Clem's eyes were wide, and his face looked stricken. "Well, you know how it is on them TV shows, back out of there and for Pete's sake don't touch nuthin else. I gotta use this phone for what it's really intended to do."

Clem dialed 911 and was immediately transferred to the Sheriff's Department. The bored deputy who answered the phone suddenly became animated. "You stay right there and don't touch anything. I'll call the Sheriff and get a couple of units rolling."

"They're rolling a couple of units," Clem said authoritatively.

They moved over to sit on a corrugated tin culvert that went under the small dirt road. They couldn't take their eyes off that leg and just sat staring, dumbfounded.

Billy Bob nodded somberly. "I'd expect them to send the whole dang police force."

Clem shook his head. "The police force ain't got no jurisdiction out here in the county. They're rolling Sheriff's Department units." He sat there for a minute and then added, "and they're calling the Sheriff."

Billy Bob broke away from being transfixed by the spell of the leg and turned wide eyes on his friend. "The Sheriff is coming out here?"

"Calm down; he's not coming to see us."

"That makes me no never mind. Sure wish I had me a cup of coffee or two before this place gets to be crawling with cops."

Clem sighed deeply. "Yeah, me too."

◊

Sheriff Buck Green was watching TV with his boots off when the call came in. He pulled his boots back on and slapped his silver Stetson on his head on the way out the door. He beat his first patrol car by several minutes.

Clem and Billy Bob came to some semblance of attention as his unit slid to a stop. Buck smiled as he got out. *Not the sharpest knives in the drawer*, he thought.

"Evening, boys, I understand you guys have something to show me."

Buck was a small-church pastor that ran for Sheriff a number of years back because he needed more income than his little church could provide. But he was well-loved, and everyone just naturally kept re-electing him.

Even though Buck's men dressed in chocolate-brown pants and khaki uniform shirts, he still wore the blue jeans and striped western shirt of a rancher. Only the gold badge on a leather flap hanging from his shirt pocket identified him as a law enforcement officer.

Billy Bob led the way. "It's over here, Sheriff."

"It?"

"It used to be a 'him,' but is a body still a 'him' or does it become an 'it'?"

Buck ignored the question. "You recognize him?"

"Sheriff, he's so beat up, it could be my own brother, and I wouldn't know him.'

Buck turned on the big flashlight he brought with him. It lit the scene up brightly. "What did you touch?"

"I felt for a pulse on his neck like they do on TV, but that's all. I didn't feel one, but the body was so ice-cold I knew he had to be dead." Billy Bob shivered as he remembered the clammy feel of the skin. "Clem videoed the whole thing on his phone so you can see exactly what I did.'

Buck knelt down and checked the pulse himself to find it was exactly as Billy Bob had said. "Videoed, huh? Well, aren't you guys up-to-date?"

"Maybe Clem is; I do good to just use one as a phone."

"I'll need that phone for a day or two, Clem."

"No problem, Sheriff." He handed it over. "About the only calls I get on it is from my wife anyway. I call it my 'electronic leash.' I'm surprised she hasn't already called to see why I'm not home."

Buck tucked the phone into his shirt pocket. He turned the light to get a better look at the pair, and they blinked and shrank from the glare like possums caught under a porch light. "How come you boys to be out walking on a country road this time of night?"

He could tell this was the part of the conversation they had been dreading. "I guess we might have had a beer or two too many, Sheriff. The bartender thought so anyway; he took my truck keys away from me."

Buck decided to set their minds at ease. "That's a good thing, boys. Drunk driving can land you in jail, but no law against drunk walking as long as you aren't disturbing the peace."

Clem perked up. "We sure weren't disturbing the peace. Not that there's any peace out here to disturb."

The three were suddenly illuminated by the headlights of an approaching patrol car. Buck motioned back to where the pair had been sitting. "If you boys don't mind having a seat back over there again, it's going to get a little busy here for a while."

"We don't mind," Clem said, "this is better than watching a police show on television."

◊

Chief Deputy Raul Fernandez got out of the first unit. Raul stood six-foot-five without his boots on and weighed a rock-solid 250 pounds. Years ago, when he filled out the job application to join the department, he hadn't classified himself as Hispanic, but instead noted he had been born and raised in Clear Creek. That said a lot about how he thought of himself, but his features didn't leave his heritage in doubt whether he wrote it on the form or not.

Raul had a frown on his face as he walked up to the sheriff. "Whatcha got, Buck? Dispatch said something about a body?"

Buck focused the beam of his light on the bush. "Yes, right over there. Clem and Billy Bob found him."

"So it's a 'him'?"

"Pretty banged up, but I don't know him. I don't want anybody over there until Little Bear can look at the scene. I don't want it tracked up any more than it has been. I've called him, and he said he'd be right here."

Raul pointed to some approaching headlights. "That looks like his old truck now."

Charley Little Bear was one of Buck's oldest friends. He was a full-blood Navajo. Little Bear wore his dark black hair caught up in two braids that fell below his shoulders, and his black, flat-brimmed hat sported a very colorful beaded hatband. He was even shorter than Buck but significantly outweighed him. A world-class tracker, it was said he could track an ant across solid rocks.

"Whatcha got, Buck?"

"That's exactly what Raul said. What I have is a dead guy. No, I don't know him; he was found by that brain trust sitting over on that culvert, and nobody has been near him but those two and me."

"Does it look like he died of natural causes?"

"I don't think a man can beat himself to death, and that's what it looks like has happened to him."

"Then the tracks of you three are not all the ground will have to tell me."

"That's what I'm hoping."

"I know your tracks as well as my own, Buck, let me go check out the tracks these two make, and I'll see what I can make out. Can we pull our cars over to get as much light as possible?"

While they repositioned the cars, Little Bear familiarized himself with the tracks Clem and Billy Bob made. Then he started working the ground toward the body slowly, often kneeling, using the headlights and Buck's big flashlight. He painstakingly covered the ground for almost an hour.

Finally, he returned. "Besides the three of you and the victim himself, there are two other sets of tracks unaccounted for."

"You think it's his killer or killers?"

"Unless, as you said, he beat himself to death."

CHAPTER 2

Buck looked up to see another set of headlights approaching. The town's only female deputy, Carol Tatum, got out of the driver's side with Doc Malone getting out on the other. Doc was in general practice but also served as the coroner in the small town.

He looked serious as he approached. "Whatcha got, Buck?"

Buck and Little Bear began to laugh.

Doc didn't get the joke. "What's so funny?"

"Nothing, Doc, you guys just need to develop some new material is all."

Doc looked confused. Raul said, "Both Little Bear and I said exactly the same words when we walked up."

"Well maybe it is the proper protocol for getting up to speed on something like this," he growled. "You ever think of that?"

"You may be right, Doc." Buck shook his head. "Maybe it is. Little Bear has been checking the tracks; he was about to tell us what he found."

Little Bear nodded then led them closer. "The tracks of the two who found him are clear. One of them, Clem, stopped here. The other went over and knelt by the body, as you did, Buck."

Buck nodded. "That's correct."

"That leaves two sets of tracks unaccounted for, as I said. You stepped on top of them when you approached, but that still left plenty to see. There are fresh tire tracks that go on down the road.

They came from down that way." He pointed. "I know that because when the brakes were slammed on, the skid marks that it made go toward where your cars are sitting. Whoever it was drove on out that way after killing this man."

"It never fails to amaze me how much you can read from tracks," Buck said.

"I'm just warming up."

Carol took pictures with a video camera of everything he pointed out as they went. That would make writing the report that much easier.

"Here's where the car slid to a stop. Three people got out, two men and a woman."

Surprise registered on everyone's face at the same time. "A woman?" Buck said. "I wasn't expecting a woman."

"This man was driving." He pointed to tracks coming around to what would have been the front of the car. He's a big man, maybe 240 or 250 pounds judging from the depth of the tracks and comparing them to my own. The size of his shoes generally says something about how tall he might be, and I would say he was a good-sized man, maybe six feet tall or so."

Little Bear pointed to another set of tracks. "This is your victim coming around from the passenger side of the car. You can see they came around face-to-face with one another. The victim tried to walk off going this way, but it looks like the big man caught up to him here."

Raul said, "I'm no tracker, but that looks like a pretty good scuffle to me."

"Yes, that's exactly what it is; they apparently fought all over this area." He pointed out the area of the fight with a small stick he had been using. "Then it appears the victim tried to get away by running into the brush over there, but the big man caught him and hit him with something, causing him to fall where he lay."

Buck interrupted. "You said something about a woman?"

"Yes, I can't tell you at what point in all this she got out, but she got out of the rear driver's side door and came up just past the front of the car. Before the car left, she got back in in the same place she was sitting."

Doc was incredulous. "If that don't beat all, it's almost like you were here watching it."

"On a remote road like this, and with nobody being out here since it happened, the tracks are very clear. And they tell a very clear story."

Buck cleared his throat. "Hummm, well are you through? Can Doc approach the body now?"

"The ground has told me all it has to say."

"Okay, Doc, it's all yours."

Doc knelt down and began a quick examination. He stuck a probe in to get a body temperature. He looked at the reading and grunted. "I can definitely pronounce him dead, and I'd place the time of death at around midnight, give or take an hour or so. I can't say for sure without an autopsy, but I'm fairly positive that this wound here on the back of his head is the cause of death. Some sort of round object, hollow from the shape of the markings."

"Like a pipe?" Raul said. "Or maybe a tire iron?"

"Something like that. I think we can ID your victim, his wallet is here."

He pulled the wallet and handed it to Buck, who opened it to the driver's license. "Delbert Abernathy, and it says here he's from Houston." He looked at the photo ID and at the man's face. "I'd say that was him all right. No robbery, he's got maybe three or four hundred bucks in here."

He handed the wallet to Raul. "Count that so we'll have an exact amount to log in."

Raul took the wallet, but before he began to count, he turned over the plastic picture holders and saw something else. "Sheriff, did you see this?"

Buck took it back and looked at it. "Well, well, it appears our Mr. Abernathy was a licensed Private Investigator."

◊

Buck stopped by his church on his way in to the department, just to have a moment to himself to think and organize his thoughts before he got into the hubbub of his office. He loved this old, converted one-room schoolhouse on the outskirts of town. He'd originally signed on as Deputy Sheriff to make ends meet when his small congregation couldn't pay enough to maintain a full-time pastor. Over the years, the job at the department grew until he found himself elected Sheriff. Now, his law enforcement job took so much time that his ministerial duties had become the part-time function.

Every now and then, he entertained thoughts about moving to a bigger church, one that could pay a living wage so he could minister full time. But the thoughts didn't last long. He really didn't *fit* in a big-church environment. The people in his little church were *his* kind of people. That meant he was just where he belonged.

He wandered to the pulpit, checked that the floors had been swept, and thought about the sermon he had to write for Sunday. Could he use anything from today's encounter as a lesson there?

One thing was constant here, no matter which job he was doing, he knew these people, each and every one. They went to work when they were supposed to. On Sundays, they were in their pew at church, and on Friday nights, in their seats at the high school football game. It was a pretty good life, the kind that might make folks want to move to a small town.

When people learned that he wore a badge *and* toted a Bible, they usually wanted to know which came first. No question about it; he served God, plain and simple. So far, he'd been able to do both, but in the event he couldn't, the resolution was simple. The badge came off.

◊

The little town of Clear Creek sat alone in arid West Texas. Technically, it was part of the Chihuahuan desert that extended from this area down into old Mexico. The countryside surrounding the community sat dry and flat, punctuated by low mesquite bushes (which rivaled cactus for the title of hardiest plant in the world) and by endless lines of pump jacks that sucked unceasingly at underground pools of oil.

A traffic jam in Clear Creek was not unheard of but *was* generally of very short duration. Cars would stack up in front of the post office about nine in the morning after the mail had been put up in the boxes. Around Christmas time, traffic would get heavy out by the big discount store, and it would get congested downtown right before and after the rodeo parade.

Then, of course, Friday nights late in the year, forget about being in a hurry in or out of the football stadium or, for that matter, anywhere in its general proximity.

One hundred years of cultivation and care had filled Clear Creek with green yards and tree-lined roads and parks. The pace of life moved slowly and methodically, characteristic of border communities and their Mexican neighbors.

The Sheriff's Department was in the courthouse, with the jail located on the top floor. It was an old building, and his department really needed to move out into their own facility. The county could use the office space, too. But with current budget restraints, it just wasn't in the cards. The air conditioning had been updated recently, though, and it felt deliciously cool as he walked in through the wooden double-doors. In the desert, it cooled off at night, but it didn't take long to heat up in the morning. Now mid-morning, it was already pushing ninety.

Buck stopped to let the cool wash over him. He pulled his hat off and used a bandanna from his back pocket to mop his forehead and neck. He used it to wipe the sweat from his hatband before returning it to his pocket.

He hung the hat on the rack as he went into his office and eased his bones into the old wooden office chair. The spring on the chair groaned but allowed it to go back easily, and he felt fatigue fall away as he put his feet up. He had a side desk drawer pulled open for that purpose, as he didn't like the way it looked to prop them up on top of the desk.

His secretary came in with a cup of black coffee.

"Dang it, Sue, I've told you a thousand times you don't have to bring me coffee."

Sue was a plus-sized lady with a round face and an ever-present smile. "I know that, Sheriff; I just like to do it. Surely you don't mind me spoiling you a little?"

"I do appreciate it, and I guess everybody can use a little spoiling now and then."

As she turned and left, Raul stood in the door grinning. "I don't know why you fight it, Buck, she's gonna do it no matter what you say."

"I know that, but I have to protest now and then, just to let her know I don't want to take advantage of her."

Raul eased into one of the two wooden chairs facing Buck's desk. "Figured you to hot-foot it straight over here. You stop by the church?"

Buck nodded. "That mess out there had me a little stressed. A little time talking to the Lord there in the quiet of the church makes it go away. Sometimes, when I get in that mode, I lose track of time."

"I understand that. Well, speaking of the mess out there, the forensics guy from Midland PD came over, as you asked. He went over the place pretty thoroughly, and he'll send us a report, but he didn't think he found anything that would help."

Raul grinned. "I told him about what Little Bear told us, and he was really impressed. He said he was happy to come over and help if we'd loan Little Bear to them on occasion. I said I was sure you would be glad to."

"Of course, I would. You get Billy Bob and Clem home?"

Raul laughed. "I sure did. It looked like every light was on in both houses when I drove up. They were scared of what they were about to walk into and wanted me to walk them in and explain where they had been."

"You do it?"

"Sure, and those women were mighty mad. They calmed down as soon as they saw I wasn't bringing them home drunk and explained that it was our fault they had been detained."

"They were sober?" Buck asked.

"Well, that was a pretty sobering experience, don't you think?"

"I'm glad they got off light. So, no help from the forensics guy. We have anything else yet?"

"I contacted Houston PD to ask about the victim. They knew him and said he was an okay guy with a pretty good reputation. They said he didn't do a lot of chasing husbands or taking sleazy pictures, said he wasn't that kind of investigator. His business was apparently a lot of corporate-related work."

"That surprises me." Buck scratched behind his ear. "When I saw he was a PI, I figured the man and woman were going to turn out to be a cheating husband or wife, and he got caught in the middle."

"I don't think we can rule that out. They didn't say he *never* did that, just said he didn't do *much* of it."

"You contact his office?" Buck asked.

"I did. It's just him and a secretary. She hadn't heard, and I guess they were pretty close. She was pretty torn up. It hadn't occurred to me that she hadn't gotten the word. Thinking back, I hope I wasn't too blunt; I just don't remember how I broke it to her. She was so upset that she wasn't really any help. I let it go and said I'd contact her in a couple of days."

"He have family?"

"No, I got that much out of it. Seems she was about all the family he had."

"You were right to give her some time."

"She did say when she could get her wits about her, she'd look and see if she could tell what he had been working on."

CHAPTER 3

B uck was a porch-sitter. His front porch extended the length of his house, with his favorite rocker right in the center. He had a little fridge out there, and a number of neighbors generally came over to join him in the afternoons. Two of the most regular neighbors from down the street were walking together down the walk as he sat down. Doc Malone was coming up on the porch with the newspaper publisher, Barney Hoke.

Barney didn't look much like a scrappy newspaper editor, more like an absent-minded professor. He wore a bow tie and one of his light-colored suits in either the oppressive heat of summer or the dead of winter—didn't matter to him. His totally gray hair fell over his forehead almost to his dark-rimmed glasses.

Doc had always reminded Buck of Milburn Stone, the actor who played the role of Doc on the old TV show *Gunsmoke*, in looks and in attitude. Buck smiled. He was pretty sure the comparison was something Doc did on purpose, right down to the hat always worn back on his head, the dark mustache, and the wire-rimmed glasses.

"Big doings," Barney said as he got a cold drink and sat down. Buck just nodded.

"Doc told me something about it, but of course, I know better than to use it until you clear it. We don't get a lot of big crime, but I know, sometimes, you hold things back to give you something to trip a suspect up with. I've got time before I need to go to press."

Doc started to defend himself on letting the cat out of the bag, but Buck cut him off. "It's fine, Doc. And Barney, we don't know enough yet to have anything to hold back. I don't see a problem with you letting people know that he was a Houston Private Investigator. Who knows, there might be somebody connected with what he's doing here that might come forward."

"And Little Bear placed a man and a woman there?"

"I said we had nothing to hold back, but we might keep the fact that there was a woman there to ourselves right now. I'll tell you what, though, it wouldn't hurt to give a little credit to the two good old boys that found him. I don't think I would say anything about them finding him because they were too drunk to drive. I'm afraid that might give me a couple more murders to have to investigate."

A patrol unit pulled up to the curb, and Raul and Little Bear got out. They made their way to the porch, got soft drinks and sat down. Raul pulled the tab on his drink, sucked down a significant amount of the liquid, closed his eyes and sighed heavily. "Ahhhhh. I needed that."

Doc said, "Hard day?"

"Just busy." Raul looked over at Buck. "Mrs. Simmons called back."

"Mrs. Simmons?"

"The victim's secretary."

"Oh, I don't guess I heard her name. She any help?"

"Maybe. She overnighted us the files on his open cases."

"Any of them seem to have a local connection?"

"Maybe. And there may be a connection that isn't visible."

"He charges expenses to whatever case he's working on, right? Won't that tell us which case it is?"

"Surprisingly enough, I thought of that, but she said he hasn't sent her any charge instructions for this trip yet. She has credit card charges, but nothing to say what case they would be charged to."

"Of course not, it couldn't be that easy."

◊

The following morning, Buck, Raul, and Carol sat around the desk in his office. Each had a steaming cup of coffee in hand. The files Mrs. Simmons had overnighted were in a portable file box on the desk between them. Nobody seemed to want to touch them.

Buck finally reached over to dig a file out of the box. "Guess we've got it to do."

Raul and Carol reached over to get one as well. "What are we looking for?" Carol frowned as she opened the folder.

Buck leaned his chair back and put his boots in the accustomed place in his side drawer. "Hanged if I know…something—anything—any kind of link to Clear Creek would be nice."

Raul took a long pull from his cup of coffee before he dug into his file. "We do need something; we don't have anything else going for us."

Buck looked over at him. "We get anything from the canvas of the hotels?"

"Not really. Not when all we had to go on was a big guy and a small woman. You know how many fit that bill on any given day? We got a list of anybody that fit that description over a three-day period before, during and after the day the victim was found."

That caught Carol's attention. "Any of them from Houston?"

"Two rooms showed a Houston address." Raul slid the list over to her.

Buck nodded at the list. "Let's cross-check that list against the names on these files and see if we get lucky."

He continued to read in the file he had while he waited for Raul and Carol to check the names on the files against the hotel list. "Nothing," Raul tossed the list down.

Buck smiled. "Didn't think so. Again, that would have been too easy. But keep the list handy. Remember the name on the folder is just the name of the client. We may find names of persons of interest down in the files somewhere that might give us a lead."

They sat in silence, sipping coffee and reading. After about twenty minutes, Carol said, "This file is a woman who thinks her husband is cheating on her."

"His secretary did say he did a small amount of that type work. Why does that jump out at you?"

"He's a salesman for Oilfield Services; they've got an office here." She reached over and got the hotel list. "And his name is on this hotel list, with a Houston address."

"Now that *is* mighty interesting. I believe we need to go to Houston and talk to the boy. Let's finish these files, though. We may have somebody else we need to talk to while we're there."

Buck tossed his file back on the desk and got another one. "I didn't see anything at all in there that has any sort of tie to here. Doesn't mean there isn't a tie, just that it isn't apparent."

Raul threw his file back, too. "Buck, what are the odds that there is going to be another file that has any kind of tie to us here?"

Buck thought about that one for a minute. "A long shot for sure, but at this stage of the game, we can't afford to overlook anything. There are guys in jail—put there on circumstantial evidence—who maybe shouldn't be there. Sometimes, it's just because people quit looking and focused all their efforts on the first thing they came up with. I think we got us a guy cheating on his wife all right, but that doesn't make him a murderer. I don't want us to leave a killer hiding in the weeds because we got sidetracked by the first thing we saw."

Carol frowned. "Just because he's cheating on his wife doesn't mean he *isn't* our killer either."

"No, ma'am, it sure doesn't, and for the time being, he's our best lead. I just don't want to rule out any other lead we may have."

◊

Three hours digging through files, and it seemed like all the words were running together. Buck tossed another file onto the 'dead pile.'

"I don't know about you guys, but I'm starting to think this doesn't have to be done in one sitting."

Carol looked relieved. "I was hoping you'd think of that."

Raul put a place marker in the file he was reading. "Me, too."

"You guys wanna come to the porch with me?"

Raul was a regular and nodded affirmatively. Carol had never done the porch-sitter bit with the 'guys,' but was interested. "I've never been over there. I thought it was something of a guy thing and didn't think I was invited."

Buck frowned. "You think you need to be invited? You're welcome anytime, whether I'm there or not. Various parts of the group are often there without me."

"Then I think I'd like to join you."

CHAPTER 4

Barney, Doc and Buck's nephew, Wayne Tunnell, were on the porch when the trio drove up. With the swing and some available folding chairs, the porch could seat nine or ten people easily.

Buck led Carol to the small fridge. "Nothing alcoholic if that's what you want, but there's quite a selection, and anything there is fair game."

"There's some lemonade in that pitcher," Doc said. "I made it fresh before I came over."

Carol got a glass and poured some. "That sounds wonderful."

They got drinks and settled in. "Delicious," she said. She sat there for a bit but kept looking over at the fridge. "You don't keep that locked?"

"No, there's never been a problem with that."

"No one has ever stolen anything?"

Buck shook his head. "No stealing here; if someone is thirsty, they're welcome to it."

"Amazing."

"Not only is there never a problem with things disappearing, but it accumulates drinks, and occasionally I have to move some of them to the refrigerator in the house."

"Really?"

"Let me explain, my dear," Barney said. "We don't wish to be a burden on Buck's hospitality, so we all bring new stock from time to time. Periodically, it tends to build up some."

"Oh, I see. So if I come back again…"

"Only if you want to," Buck said. "No one has ever been asked to do it."

"When I first got here, I didn't have a job or much money," Wayne said. "I got drinks here all the time, and nobody ever said a word. Of course, now that I'm working, I contribute to the cause."

"But enough of that, Carol," Doc saluted her with his drink. "We are so pleased to have you join us. This porch has seen an over-abundance of testosterone."

Carol laughed. "Surely I'm not the first woman?"

"No, my dear, not the first, but it is a rare occurrence nonetheless. And a great pleasure."

"So, Buck," Barney said, "anything new on the murder?"

"Still early." Without giving any names or information, he told them about the three of them digging through the PI's files.

"That doesn't sound very exciting."

Buck shrugged. "Much of police work is that way—boring stakeouts, digging through records, just looking for those loose ends that we can pick at until one of them turns into a lead."

"But you think it is going to lead you to Houston?"

"Absolutely, but we want to make sure we have all the leads we need to follow up on before we go."

"We?" Carol's eyebrows went up.

"Yes, we. If I go, as the Chief Deputy, Raul will be in charge here, but I'll need help." He smiled. "Besides, I may need protection."

Everyone snickered at that one. They all knew Carol's martial arts prowess. Several were there when she took the town bully apart without even breaking a sweat. From that point on, no one thought of her as a "token" officer.

"When are we going?"

"We have to dig through that box of files first."

◊

There were no pews in Buck's little church; the congregation sat in padded folding chairs. They didn't match since they had been added to and replaced many times over the years. It would hold eighty or ninety people but was generally pretty full for services.

The pulpit was simple, built by Buck and one of his deacons, and wasn't on a raised platform, but on the floor in the front. A nice upright piano stood at the front, half facing the congregation. It had been a gift from the Widow Jacobson when she got too old to play. The chore of leading the music was shared by several different people, as was the singing of special music.

It was an older congregation, drawn to the little church by Buck's no-nonsense preaching and his straight-from-the-Bible teaching. Truth be known, many of those who came there were refugees from contemporary services at much larger churches that had gotten a bit loud for their hearing aids.

Buck looked out over the congregation. It was again a full house. He spent time working up sermons, but sometimes, even after all that preparation, he didn't use them if the Lord put something else on his heart to say. That was the case this morning.

He admitted it to those assembled, "You folks know how I am.

Sometimes the Lord puts it on me to speak on something other than what I have planned. I've even come up here with sermon notes in front of me, and when I opened my mouth, have gone somewhere else entirely."

He saw nothing but smiling faces; they knew all about it. "That's the way it is this morning. Listening to the radio while I was getting ready, it occurred to me that there is a gulf between Christians and politics. You know I often wrestle with the conflict of serving both the Bible and the badge, and we talk about that a lot."

The smiles were still there, but he could tell they were wondering where he was going with this. "Listening to the news, it occurred to me that as Christians, we have the same sort of problem as to our role regarding politics. Some of the strongest Christians I know refuse to be drawn in at all, saying God is in charge, and He is going to take care of everything."

He could see a number of frowns now. "Now I admire that kind of faith, powerful faith, but it's a little misguided. God *is* in charge, and everything that happens in the way our country is being governed, He either ordains, or He allows. All through the years, Israel alternated between being strong and faithful and going off chasing after other gods. I never really understood how they could allow themselves to be seduced that way."

Nodding. They were with him there. "But God works through His children. Refusing to be involved in the way we are governed, or not going to vote, is taking a pair of His hands off the battlefield. The Great Commission tells us we are to go forth and witness, to tell all the world. I believe we are also to be a good example and to try to affect the morality of the world around us."

He came around the pulpit to close the distance. He knew that drew him closer to them in more than just space. "It seems the government is dead-set on taking God out of the classrooms, out of the public marketplace, out of every aspect of our lives. I don't blame them; I blame *us*! Christians have laid back and kept quiet too long. Many do it because they buy into the fallacy of separation of church and state. That doesn't mean Christians don't have a say, it means the government is not supposed to infringe on our religious liberty."

He smiled. "I know this is not my usual type of sermon. Oh, I do border on politics now and then, but listening to that radio this morning, I heard a clarion call to battle. I heard the Lord telling me we weren't engaging for Him. I think it's a call we all need to heed."

Buck shifted into closing remarks and gave an altar call not expecting any results, particularly given the topic of his sermon. That and the fact that he was pretty sure of the standing of most of his congregation. Still, you never could tell, and he believed strongly that you should never pass up a chance to offer people the opportunity to follow Jesus just in case…

◊

It was strange that one of Buck's best friends wasn't a Christian. Doc was an agnostic. He wasn't a disbeliever, but he wasn't a dedicated follower either. Buck could never be sure whether he had more faith than he exhibited or he just liked to play devil's advocate and critique his friend or engage Buck in discussion. Whatever the case, Doc was probably the most faithful attendee of the services.

They usually went to eat after services, and then, as on most other days, they would end up on the front porch. Barney attended over at First Baptist, and as usual when he came up on the porch, tried to stir things up by asking Doc, "How'd he do today?"

Doc looked serious and said, "Not bad, not bad at all. Course I couldn't really tell whether he was preaching to his flock or running for office."

"Oh, really?"

"He told the congregation that Christians have an obligation to serve the Lord by trying to affect the world around them, and it included being involved in politics."

"I can't argue with that. Of course, that should mean paying close attention to what they read in the newspaper."

Doc snorted. "You going to talk about the sermon or try to hawk papers?"

Barney looked over at Buck. "You agree with his assessment?"

"Pretty much what I said all right."

"How does that jive with the beatitudes, you know, the meek shall inherit the earth sort of thing?"

"Meek is an attitude, Barney, it refers to being calm and not boisterous in dealing with people. I don't think it means we have to get pushed around or have to give up our say."

CHAPTER 5

Monday morning, an ever-present cup of java in hand, Buck sat looking at the still large number of case files in the file box. His cohorts joined him, and they looked at them over the top of their cups, willing themselves to dig in and start the process.

Penny, the dispatcher, stuck her head in the door. "Sheriff, we've got a domestic disturbance call out on Parker road."

Saved by the bell. "Parker road? Outside the city limits, so that makes it county."

They knew Buck felt he should be involved in domestic disturbance calls because of the counseling aspect. Normally, law enforcement people hated having to catch such a call because of the possibility of violence and because they never knew what they were walking into.

Raul said, "You want me to go with you?"

He reached for his hat. "I think I'll take Carol, you know, for the female perspective?"

Not that Buck wouldn't like to have Raul's size if things got rough, but with Carol's martial arts ability, he wasn't giving up much there anyway.

Raul sighed. "That leaves me stuck with these files."

Buck laughed. "You can wait until we get back if you want."

Raul reached into the box. "No, I might as well get on it; it has to be done.

They drove quickly out to the address, lights, but no siren. As they drove up, they saw a couple on the porch. The man was standing over a woman lying on the floor, hand to her forehead palm out.

Carol was out of the car almost before it stopped rolling, and before Buck could get out, she was standing between the couple facing the man.

"Get out of here," the man snarled. "This is none of your business."

Buck moved up behind the man. "I think you've made it our business."

"Get this broad out of my face before I give her some of the same."

"That would be the biggest mistake you ever made, friend, and I don't think she plans to go anywhere. Suppose you step over here and let's talk."

"I said move, woman," the man growled.

He reached for Carol's shirtfront. She grabbed his wrist, and with one quick movement, had his arm pinned behind him and shoved him down to his knees.

Buck moved over to help the woman up. There were several places on her face beginning to color up. "Are you all right?"

"I'm okay, Sheriff. We don't want no trouble."

"Looks to me like you have trouble whether you want it or not."

She looked at her husband with concern in her face, or was it fear? "Roger is okay; he just lost his temper is all."

"He lose his temper often?"

"Now and then."

Buck frowned. "How come you've never called us?"

She looked down at the floor. "We handle our own problems."

He helped her sit down. "Doesn't look like you're handling them very well."

The man's rage was escalating. "Let go of me or I'll rip your head off."

That was too good to pass up, so Carol let go of him and stepped back. "Oh, really? You like to hit women, do you? Is that because they don't hit back?"

Roger came up off the floor with a guttural roar. Carol side-stepped him easily, hooked a hand in his armpit and pulled him into a hip-lock that threw him up over her back and clear off the porch. He landed flat on his back, and Buck could hear all the air go out of him.

He got up slowly, painfully, more cautious now.

"You're not too bright, are you, Roger?" Buck said.

The enraged man threw a huge roundhouse punch at Carol. She ducked under easily and hit him with four or five quick jabs, each rocking his head back. They came so fast, Buck was unsure of the number.

"I think you need to quit while you still have your senses, Roger," Buck said.

The man wiped away a fleck of blood with the back of his hand. "I'm just warming up."

"Then I think it's time to cool you off. Carol, I know you're enjoying this, but I think it's time to put a stop to it."

"Yes, sir."

Carol jumped into the air, spun, and brought her right foot around in a tight arc, all her weight behind it. Roger again landed flat on his back. This time, he did not get up.

The woman's hand went to her mouth. "Is...is he dead?"

Buck smiled. "No, but I expect he'll be able to match you bruise for bruise."

"I'm not pressing charges, Sheriff."

"You don't have to. He did it out in plain sight; we don't need anyone pressing charges." He motioned to all the people standing on nearby porches. "And I'd say we have plenty of witnesses. One of them probably called it in. And now we have assaulting a police officer to add to the charges."

He looked at Carol. "Cuff him."

◊

The man, now identified as Roger Walker, sat at the table in the stark little interrogation room at the Sheriff's Department. Raul and the Sheriff looked at him through the small pane of one-way glass.

Raul couldn't believe it. "So he tried to do some of his woman-beating stuff on Carol, huh?"

Buck grinned. "I tried to warn him, twice."

"Some people gotta learn the hard way." He turned to look at Buck. "You think he learned?"

"Not a chance. But the lesson is still in progress. I went out prepared to do a little counseling at his house. I reckon he has to sit still for it now."

Buck went next door. Walker was still in cuffs, which were

attached to a loop on the conference table. He raised the cuffs up for show. "You must think I'm a real dangerous guy."

"So far, you haven't exactly shown yourself to be a pussycat." Buck sat down across the table from him. "Besides, I'm getting too old to wrestle around with prisoners if I don't have to, and I don't have to. You give me any trouble, and I'll take those cuffs off and call Carol in to take you to jail."

"She just got in a lucky punch. It ain't fair fighting with your feet."

"I've got news for you, she'll get a lucky punch in any time you go at her, and you can take that to the bank."

"Humph!"

Buck leaned forward, putting his elbows on the table. "I want to talk to you a little about what happened today."

Walker leaned away from Buck in a sort of insolent pose. "I don't have to talk until my lawyer gets here."

"No, you sure don't, and we've sent for him as you asked. And if you don't want to talk that's okay with me. I'll do the talking, and you can sit there and pretend you aren't listening, but that's really hard to do when you have no choice but to sit there."

Behind the one-way glass, Walker's lawyer stood talking with Raul, sizing up his client before he went in to see him. Mike Donovan represented the man's boss, mostly in business matters.

He looked at Raul. "Well, isn't he a sweetheart?"

Raul nodded. "He seems to take a lot of pleasure in hitting women."

"Looks like he has no choice but to sit and listen to Buck until I get there."

"That's how it works."

"I'm in no hurry. I haven't had my coffee yet, and I hate to have to go through this without it."

"How about we go get a cup, and then you can go in? We can use Buck's office."

"I warn you, it takes me a while for me to drink a cup of coffee. I just nurse at it a little until it cools enough to drink."

"I'll make sure it's *real* hot."

◊

Buck sat for a while looking at Walker before he said, "Let me guess. Your daddy never told you that a real man *never* hits a woman… under any circumstances."

"I never knew who my daddy was."

"Now why am I not surprised? Let me try another guess. There was a lot of physical abuse in your home growing up?"

"If you mean did my old lady beat me? Yes, all the time." Roger said. "Besides, there was always some old boy hanging around, and a lot of them beat on her. She'd take it out on me."

"Sounds to me like you aren't really beating your wife, you're beating your mother."

"That's a stupid thing to say, and I said I wasn't talking to you until my lawyer gets here."

"That's up to you."

Buck sat there looking at the man. A cycle of abuse like this was very hard to break. "I don't suppose you know that, in addition to being the Sheriff, I'm also the pastor of a small church?"

Walker's eyebrows went up in surprise. "No kidding? How

does that work?"

"A lot of people ask me that, but I don't have a problem with doing both. I told you that so you wouldn't be surprised when I told you it looks to me like life has handed you a pretty raw deal."

"Is that the preacher talking?"

"No, the Sheriff sees the same thing. But the law enforcement officer is likely to think you need to be locked up until you see the error of your ways. The preacher is sitting here wondering if your name is written in the Lamb's Book of Life."

Walker screwed his face up. "Lamb's Book? What's that supposed to be?"

"It means have you ever been saved?"

He cocked his head. "Saved from what?"

"That tells me the answer right there."

"You aren't making any sense."

Buck held a hand out, palm up. "Let me ask you this: do you believe there's a heaven?"

"I'd like to believe there is. I mean, I'd kinda like to believe this isn't all there is and then it's a long dirt nap from now on."

"Do you think you're going there?"

"No."

"Why not?"

Walker smiled a crooked smile. "You have to ask that? I know you've seen my rap sheet by now; I ain't exactly been a boy scout."

"It's not how bad you've been, and you can't earn it by how much good you can do. Your ticket to heaven is a gift. We're all sinners, all fall short of what God would have us be. But God can't allow sin into heaven, so he sent his son to die on the cross to redeem us from our sin. It isn't what we do or don't do, but what he did for us."

"You really are a preacher, aren't you?" The words came out sarcastically.

"I am."

Walker swatted at the air as if he were warding the statement away. "Well, I've heard about that hanging on the cross thing, and it sounds like a fairy tale to me."

"Well, you've heard about heaven, have you also heard about hell?"

"I'd believe in hell before I'd believe in heaven," Walker said. "Matter of fact, I'm not sure I'm not already in hell."

"Oh no, you would surely know the difference; hell is a terrible place. The problem is that there is going to be no 'dirt nap,' as you put it. God provided us all with eternal life, and we're going to spend it either in heaven or in hell."

Walker laughed. "You saying I'm not going to die? That's stupid."

"Of course, you're going to die; we all die. But that's just the death of your physical body. Once you do, your soul is going to go through one door or the other."

"That sounds like a load of crap."

"There's a third choice."

"Really?"

"You have to choose to believe in Jesus to get to heaven. The third choice is to do nothing. Unfortunately, that choice works out to be the same as choosing to go to hell. You see, God doesn't send anybody to hell; it's a free-will choice. You either choose to go to heaven or the default is to go the other direction. The decision is yours."

Walker half-turned in his chair. "Well, my decision is to not talk to you about this."

"You keep saying that. I told you you've been handed a pretty raw deal in this life, but you can turn it around if you want to. If you did, the last thing you would want to do is hit your wife. But just in case you aren't smart enough to see the amazing gift that you're being offered, I'm here to tell you that beating your wife is over with anyway."

"How do you figure that?"

"I know the judge; you're looking at a minimum of 90 days for the charges against you, which by the way now include assaulting a police officer."

Walker touched a hand tentatively to his bruises. "It felt more like she assaulted me."

"Kinda looked that way to me, too, but you were dumb enough to start it. Anyway, 90 days is plenty of time for Carol to work with your wife on how to protect herself. She taught those skills to Marines while she was in the service, and I guarantee by the time you get out, if you raise a hand to your wife, she'll do the same thing to you that Carol did."

"You can't do that."

"It's already being done. Where do you think your wife is?"

"Oh, man."

"You better think about the things that I've told you," Buck said. "If you want to talk more about it, send word down to me, you're going to be in the jail right upstairs. I'll be happy to come talk anytime."

The door opened, and Donovan walked in. "Mr. Walker, I'm Mike Donovan. Your boss sent me here to represent you."

"Well, you took your own sweet time."

"I had a lot to do."

CHAPTER 6

As Buck went back around to his office, he noted Raul was still reading files at his own desk. "Come on in, and we'll get back to work on those," Buck said in passing.

"You have someone waiting on you first."

"Oh?"

By that time, Buck was at his office door. A tall, slender man got up and extended his hand. "Hello, Buck."

Buck shook it. "James. Have a seat. What can I do for you?"

James Ferguson sat back down. "More like what I can do for you."

"How's that?" The old chair gave a creak as Buck settled into it.

"I read about the murder in the paper and about how the guy was a private investigator. I figured I'd save you some time and tell you he was doing some work for us."

"That so? What kind of work?" Buck motioned for Raul, and as he stuck his head in the door, said, "See if we have a file for Ferguson Supply in that box." He looked back at Ferguson. "Sorry, go on."

"We've been losing a lot of oilfield supplies—drill pipe and drill bits, that kind of thing. The money adds up quickly. When rigs need supplies, they need them fast, and we aren't open 24 hours a day. Generally, if they have to come get something, they're pretty good about signing it out so it can be charged, but somebody has been taking advantage of that."

"Let me guess. Abernathy was looking into it for you?"

"He was. He was trying to find out who had been doing it, and was going to make some security recommendations for the future."

"Why didn't you file a complaint on it?"

"We're in the city limits; I filed one with the police department."

"A small town like Clear Creek doesn't have much of a police department. A Police Chief and a couple of officers. They do mostly traffic and security around town trying to prevent petty theft. They aren't really set up for investigation."

"I should have filed it over here, too, I suppose. I figured you guys worked together."

"We're always happy to support their department, but I'm afraid the chief, Sam Jackson, is pretty protective of his turf. That's pretty common in law enforcement."

Raul came in. "There's a file."

"I've got the general gist of it. You looked at it yet?"

"No, hadn't gotten down to it or I'd have let you know there's a local connection."

"Sit down and join us." He looked back to Ferguson. "So he was here working for you?"

"I don't know. I hadn't talked to him. He's on the case, but I can't say for sure that's why he was in town."

"Has he given you any progress reports on it?"

"He said he had some leads but hasn't told me anything specific."

"Well, I wouldn't think a little theft would be cause for

murder."

Ferguson smirked. "I guess that would depend on your definition of 'little.' Drilling supplies are expensive. It doesn't take long to get well up into the six figures."

Buck whistled. "I had no idea. That could sure be motive all right. Well, give us a few hours to get up to speed on this, and we'll see what we can do and whether it plays a role in the murder investigation, as well. I can tell you one thing without even looking into it."

"What's that?"

"The amount of money you told me you lost? You could have 24-Hour security for a fraction of that amount and give them jobs you'd like to have done in the process."

"Don't know why I haven't already done that." Ferguson put his hands on the arm of his chair to get up but paused. "While I'm here, you have one of my employees. Do I need to post bail or anything?"

"You're talking about Walker?"

"Yes, I understand he has problems at home, but he's been a dependable worker."

Buck hesitated. "Can I shoot straight with you? I think there might be hope for Walker's domestic problems, but it wouldn't hurt for him to be separated from his wife for a bit. No real point in trying to bail him out before his court appearance this afternoon and my guess is he's gonna be doing 90 days for assaulting an officer. Now whether this affects his job or not . . ."

"I don't know. As I said, he's a good worker. I know he drinks, but it's never affected his work. Doing some drinking is not exactly unheard of in the oilfield."

Buck laughed. "No, it's sure not."

Ferguson got to the door, but Buck stopped him by saying, "You think there's any chance Walker could be involved in your thefts? Or even in the murder?"

"Oh, no, I wouldn't think so." Ferguson appeared to be thinking about it. "But then, I know little about him except what I see on the job site."

"We can't afford to discount the idea right now. I'm thinking he just graduated to the suspect list."

◊

A little later, Raul came back in. "I finished reading that file. Abernathy was suspicious of Walker in connection with the thefts, but doesn't seem to have any proof."

"Now that's downright interesting. We may have to have another talk with the boy."

"I understand you may have introduced him to the idea of having a little faith in your last talk. Aren't you afraid you'll undo that?"

"The two shouldn't have anything to do with each other. In fact, it might just mean he needs to get right with the Lord all that much more."

Raul got up. "Well, it's time to take him over to face the judge so . . ."

Buck got out of his chair as well. "I think I'll do that myself."

"You?"

"Might give us that little chance to talk."

Raul went out to get him. "I'll have somebody bring him down. You want them to go with you?"

Buck looked offended. "The day I can't handle a prisoner in handcuffs I'll hang up my badge."

Raul grinned. "I wouldn't say that, Sheriff. I remember when the Rogers brothers nearly whipped the entire department, and they had cuffs on."

Buck grimaced. "Couldn't forget that if I tried, but they were built like Mack trucks. Walker sure ain't in their league."

"But Walker does have a history of violence."

"I haven't heard of him taking anybody on that would fight back. He seems to confine his violence to women who are defenseless."

Raul smiled. "Carol may have broken him of doing that."

"I'm counting on it…and on the self-defense lessons she's giving to his wife."

The door from the stairwell to the jail opened. "Here's your chance; there he is."

The Sheriff's Department shared the ground floor with several other county offices. The courtroom and other offices were on the second floor, and the jail occupied the entire top floor. Two staircases accessed the second floor, but a single secure staircase accessed the jail with no stop on the second floor. It was the only point of entry other than the outside fire escape.

Buck took charge of the prisoner and walked him up to the courtroom. Another trial had just finished, and the room was empty except for the judge, the bailiff, and the court reporter. As they entered the courtroom, the judge waved them forward.

"Good morning, Judge," Buck said as they approached.

"Morning. Is this man not represented by an attorney?"

"I'm here, Judge." Donovan rushed into the room, out of breath.

"Mr. Donovan, I'm surprised to see you. You don't usually handle this sort of case."

"No, your honor. His employer is a client of mine and wished me to handle this for him."

"Very well, how does your client plead?"

"Guilty, your honor, and he wishes to waive his right to a jury trial."

"Good decision. With the evidence I see before me, a trial would be a waste of time. I don't see where the wife has signed a complaint on the abuse charges?"

Buck nodded. "No, your Honor, we are only proceeding on the charges of assault on a police officer."

The Judge looked at the bruises starting to turn purple and smiled. "It would appear that did not go well for him."

"No, your Honor, you know Carol. It didn't go well at all. I tried to warn him, but he seems to like hitting women."

"I think we'll see if 90 days in the cooler will give him time to think about that. Counselor, do you have anything to add before I pass sentence?"

"No, your Honor, it's pretty cut and dried."

The Judge banged his gavel. "I sentence you to 90 days in the county jail. Court is adjourned."

◊

Buck didn't immediately take Walker back upstairs. He didn't take him to the interrogation room either, but settled him into his office then returned with a couple of cups of coffee. Raul followed him in with a cup of his own.

Buck took a seat and a long drink of coffee. "That's good stuff."

Walker eyed him suspiciously over the rim of his own cup. "What are we doing, Sheriff?"

"I just thought you might like to relax a little before you have to go back to lockup."

"Somehow, this doesn't feel relaxing."

"Have you thought any more about the things we talked about?"

"The religion thing? I'll admit it has been on my mind, actually quite a bit."

"I'm going to send a Bible up to you. It'd be good if you read in it some. I'd suggest reading in the Book of Romans."

"A book inside a book? I don't understand."

Buck came around to show him the table of contents in the front of a Bible. "It's organized a little differently. It's made up of separate books written by different people and each have chapters in them. In a modern book, it is more like it has chapters with scenes in them, but don't let that put you off. It will soon make sense."

"I guess I got nothing but time."

"There is that. I don't know if you've heard anything about it or not, but we're investigating a murder."

"That Private Eye out of Houston?"

"Yes."

"I heard."

"Did you know he was investigating thefts at the place where you work?"

Walker paused, weighing his words. "This is starting to sound a lot like an interrogation."

"That doesn't answer my question."

"Yes, I knew, and I knew he was measuring me for it."

"Was he right?"

"Not that I'd cop to it if he was, but you can believe me when I tell you I had nothing to do with it."

Buck measured him with his eyes. He considered himself a good judge of character, and the man retuned his look openly with no apparent sign of evasion. Still, some people were very accomplished at lying.

"If you look in his files, I'm betting he checked on where I was every time a theft occurred and couldn't find a time when I couldn't prove where I was at the time."

"That's unusual. If you came to me wanting me to alibi myself for any particular time or place, there'd be times when I wouldn't know or couldn't prove it. How about you, Raul?"

"There'd be times even this week that if I had to produce an alibi, I'd be pressed to do it. Unusual for a guy to have one every time it was needed."

"You saying you don't believe me?"

Buck shook his head. "Nope, just wondering out loud. Guess it's time to take you up, however; you don't seem to be relaxing much anymore." He picked the Bible back up. "Take this up with you. Actually, it's a New Testament."

"A New Testament?"

"It's the last half of the Bible. It has the part in it that it would do you the most good to read right now. And the way things are going, you need the help. You just send word down if you want to talk about it…or about anything else."

CHAPTER 7

B uck sighed. "We need to finish going through these files so we can do that follow up in Houston."

Buck, Carol and Raul each took a file and settled in. Not that there wasn't something in the ones they had already looked at that they were missing, but they had found two definite connections and needed to know if they could find more.

Raul looked across the desk. "So far, I'm still thinking that cheating husband is the main contender. You know how often a 'crime of passion' gets out of hand."

Buck had to agree. "It's been known to happen all right."

Carol shook her head. "Not me; I think Walker is the key."

Buck had a barely perceptible smile on his face as he looked at her. "Not surprised you feel that way; I know he's not one of your favorite people. Speaking of which, how is his wife coming along with her training?"

"She's really throwing herself into it. By the time he gets out, she'll be ready. I just hope she doesn't pick a fight just to get the chance to kick his butt."

Buck snickered. "That'd be interesting. It'd be something if we had to arrest *her* for abuse. Well, we better get to it."

Raul said, "This PI was a worker. This is a lot of files."

"They cover quite a period of time, though. We have no way of knowing which ones he might have been doing some work on. Just because there's no recent entry doesn't mean one might have suddenly heated up."

They settled in to read. It was hard to focus on it with no sound but the hum of the air conditioning and the rustling of pages turning. More than once, Buck realized his eyes had closed on him.

Quite some time had passed before Carol said, "This may be something."

Buck's feet came down, and he sat upright. "Whatcha got?"

"The Bar-S Ranch."

"That was Jiggs Silbee's place. He died some time ago."

"Exactly. There's apparently a big flap over just who owns what."

"The ranch is in the county. Who hired Abernathy?"

"Says here it was the widow, Helen Silsbee."

"Helen. I'm surprised."

"You know her?"

"Very well, for many years. We best go out and talk to her."

"Not that easy, Sheriff. It also says here she's not living on the place. She's at her son Harold's house."

"I hadn't heard that. Where does he live?"

"That's just it. He lives in Houston."

◊

They finished the files without finding another obvious connection then adjourned to Buck's porch for a cold one. They arrived to find Doc and Barney already there. Buck spoke to them as he stepped up on the porch. "Afternoon, Doc...Barney."

Barney looked up. "We're busting with curiosity, Buck."

"Is that my neighbor talking or the newspaper?"

"It's your neighbor right now. We'll talk about what the newspaper can say later."

Buck pulled a drink from the fridge, and the three sat down. He propped his feet up on the trash can that sat in the middle and pushed his hat back on his head. "Okay, I'm comfortable, Barney. Let fly with the questions."

"Not questions; just one. You have any leads on the murder case?"

"Can't give you any names."

"No, of course not, I wouldn't expect you to."

"Well, let me put it like this; right now our suspects are a cheating husband, a major oilfield theft, and a squabble over a ranch estate. There might still be something else in those files we've been going through, but we didn't see anything obvious."

Doc said, "That's a right interesting assortment. Just off the top, with a PI involved, the cheating husband is who I'd put my money on."

Raul held up his soda. "That's what I said, Doc."

Barney shook his head. "No, I'd have to say it would be the oilfield angle. A lot of people who work in the oilfield play pretty rough."

Carol smiled. "I know about how rough they play. I haven't forgotten a bunch of hard hats fighting over at the bar that time. Anyway, that's where I'm betting."

Raul chuckled. "There's at least one of those hard hats that sure hasn't forgotten you either." He toasted her with his glass.

She smiled and returned the salute.

Buck looked surprised. "Nobody liking the ranch estate

problems?"

Barney nodded. "You do have a point there; whole wars have been fought over land. So what's the next step?"

"Carol and I are going to Houston to see if we can find some answers. Right now, all we have are questions."

"So what can I put in the paper?"

"No specifics on the leads, it might alert the wrong people. But you can say we do have some leads and are pursuing them."

"That's pretty thin for a story."

"I'll make it up to you when we have something firm."

◊

"Pack for 3-4 days," Buck said. "I'll pick you up in the morning."

"Yes, sir. Sheriff, do I wear my uniform?"

"No, we won't be looking to attract attention. Nothing too dressy, but we might eat out some place nice if that helps you plan."

"You know your way around Houston?"

"Not very well, but the Harris County Sheriff is a friend of mine. He said he'd give us a little help for a couple of days to facilitate us finding our way around the city."

"That'll be helpful."

"Anything you want to do while we're there?" Buck asked.

"No, I'm not much of a tourist type. I'm just going to be there to do what you need me to do."

"I have to warn you, for me, traveling is all about getting to eat places I don't normally get to eat in. We'll eat very well while we're out, and the county is buying, so you don't have to worry about the expense."

"I sure don't mind eating good food."

"We'll drive over and fly out of Midland. There'll be a layover in Dallas for a couple of hours."

"Most of the flying that I've done has been military," she said. "When they shipped me somewhere it wasn't exactly first class accommodations."

"Don't get the wrong idea, Carol, we won't be flying first class."

"Compared to the belly of a military transport plane, believe me, it'll *seem* like first class."

◊

Buck pulled up in front of Carol's house in his pickup. He barely had time to come to a stop before she came out pulling a small black rolling suitcase.

"Morning, Sheriff."

"Good morning, Carol."

She put her bag in the back with his and slipped into the passenger side. When Buck hired her, she was fresh out of the Marines and still in uniform. The few times he had seen her out of uniform, she had been in workout clothes or jeans. He realized he had never seen her nicely dressed. She had on a simple dress and had her hair down instead of pulled up under her hat. Her legs were sculpted and tanned. It just hadn't occurred to him what a beautiful young lady she was, but he realized it now.

"Sheriff, what's the matter? Why are you looking at me like

that?"

"I was just caught a little off guard. I guess I'm an old enough man that I can tell you I hadn't noticed what a beautiful young lady you are, but it's pretty hard to overlook now. I reckon, at my age, I can tell you without you thinking I'm hitting on you."

She laughed. "Why, Sheriff, you aren't *that* old."

"Apparently, I am, being as how it took me this long to see it."

CHAPTER 8

As they came out of the jetway at Houston, Buck saw a deputy holding a sign that said "Sheriff Green." He was a young man, slim, and his uniform looked new and was just the opposite of those Buck's deputies wore, a chocolate-colored shirt and khaki pants.

"I'm Green," he said.

"Yes, sir, I'm deputy Duckworth, Floyd Duckworth."

"This is my deputy, Carol Tatum."

Duckworth looked surprised. "*Your*..." Then he caught himself, lifted his hat and said, "Glad to meet you, ma'am."

She caught it. "Don't think anything about it. I don't suppose I look much like a deputy out of uniform. But the Sheriff doesn't want to attract attention."

"It's not working, ma'am; you'd attract attention anywhere."

Buck fought back a smile. "That did occur to me on the way here. But then I thought there's a difference between being attractive and being recognized as peace officers."

They picked up their bags and walked out to the patrol car in the no-parking loading zone. Buck noticed it and said, "Handy."

"There are a few perks involved with wearing the badge."

Buck looked at Carol and quietly said, "Don't get any ideas. It'd be bad PR in a town our size."

"Never gave it a thought."

"Well, unless there was a *reason* to need the unit right there handy."

The deputy laughed. "Like maybe saving a twenty-minute shuttle ride to the remote parking lot, another fifteen getting it out and another ten through the traffic before we're even out of the airport?"

"Point taken."

The patrol car slid easily through the traffic even without lights and siren, which Buck wouldn't permit. Still, the freeway traffic was heavy.

"I thought we were getting here at an off-peak time," Buck said.

Duckworth laughed. "There is no off-peak time in Houston. Even at three or four in the morning, these freeways will be full."

"How long have you been with the department, son?"

He looked a little embarrassed. "I'm still a rookie, sir, that's how the Sheriff could spare me so easy. But I was born and raised here and know the city like the back of my hand, so I can easily get you anywhere you need to go. I have rooms reserved for you out on the Katy Freeway. That's also Interstate 10, and it goes through the area of town where the people you need to talk to live. It's where your victim had his office as well."

Twenty minutes later, they pulled into what appeared to be a townhouse. Buck looked surprised. "This doesn't look like a hotel to me."

"No, sir. It isn't. Companies rent places like these for executives that are just moving to town, until they get located, or maybe for some people they are bringing in for a while on a temporary basis. The owner is a strong supporter of our Sheriff and is providing it to you free of charge."

"That's mighty nice, but we can just go to a hotel."

"Sheriff Everly wouldn't hear of it."

"Well, we really appreciate it."

"I'll let you get settled in and rest up a bit. I'll be back in a couple of hours and will be at your deposal. And before you say it, I know you can just take a cab but once again..."

"I know, Jerry wouldn't hear of it. Can I ask a favor?"

"Of course."

"When you return, does your department have some unmarked cars you could use?"

"Of course."

"And could you lose that uniform for the duration?"

"Yes, sir. I had already planned on that since you want to keep a low profile."

◊

Their accommodations turned out to be a two-story townhouse with two bedrooms on the second floor and a dedicated garage out back. It was furnished with towels and linens, dishes and everything one would need to move in for any length of time.

Carol came down the stairs freshened up and wearing a pantsuit. Buck smiled. "This new look takes some getting used to."

Buck still wore his usual jeans and western shirt, but now had a western-cut sports coat with a black yoke on as well as a string tie. "I've been checking out the area. You won't believe it, but there's a wooded area between us and the interstate to buffer the noise. But if we walk through those woods, we come out at an intersection and the building where Abernathy had his office is right on the other side of the highway. I thought we might leave a note for the Deputy telling him where we are and then take a little walk over there."

"Yes, sir, lead on."

The walk through the woods was pleasant, it was easy to cross under the interstate, and they found the office easily on the ground floor of the Memorial Park office building. They walked into a small but very nice office that had a lobby area, a private office, and what looked like a combination file room and workroom. A pleasant, middle-aged lady sat at the desk in the lobby area. The nameplate on her desk said she was Florence Simmons.

"Mrs. Simmons, my name is Buck Green."

"That would be Sheriff Green, I presume?"

He reached across the desk to shake her hand. "Just call me Buck. This is my deputy, Carol Tatum."

"Glad to meet you. How may I be of service?"

"I'm a little surprised the office is open. This was a one-man operation, right?"

"Yes, and I suppose I may just about be out of a job, but Mrs. Abernathy wants it kept open until she sees whether someone might want to purchase it or not. It *is* a rather high-profile office with an active client base. It might well have value to someone."

"I can see where it would. And if they have any sense, I would assume they would want to retain someone that knew the status of all the cases and all the particulars of the office."

"That's what I'm hoping, assuming it is someone I am willing to work for. In the meantime, since the office is open and I am being paid to work, please accept this as your office while you are here and don't hesitate to call on me for any support. With Mrs. Abernathy's compliments."

"That's why I put you where I did," a voice behind them said. They turned to see Deputy Duckworth standing in the door. "Convenient, wouldn't you say?"

Duckworth had changed to some khaki Docker pants and a comfortable looking brown knit shirt. He looked like a college kid straight off the campus. Buck couldn't help but notice however that his outfit still approximated the color scheme of his deputy's uniform. The kid had all the makings of a career officer.

"I would indeed," Buck said. "Okay, first things first, a rancher friend of mine always feeds a new hand before he puts him to work. Says it gets them off on the right foot. Carol can tell you when I travel it always involves trying out some good places to eat. Mrs. Simmons, would you care to join us for lunch?"

"I'd be delighted."

"This is your neck of the woods, Mrs. Simmons, do you have a recommendation?"

"If you are looking for something different to try, I suggest the Blue Star Oriental Restaurant over by Memorial Mall."

"I've never had oriental food, but it's on my bucket list to do, so let's give it a shot."

They loaded into the Deputy's unmarked car and drove the few blocks to the restaurant. They were soon seated in a booth with an assortment of food from the buffet in front of them.

"I'm flying blind here," Buck admitted. "I don't know what any of this stuff is, but it looks and smells mighty good."

He started with something he recognized, a miniature corn dog. He put a healthy dollop of mustard on it and took a big bite. Just before it entered his mouth, Duckworth said loudly, "Sheriff, that's…"

But it was too late.

It wasn't a corn dog as Buck thought, and the mustard was nothing like any mustard he had ever experienced before. His head lit up, and his throat was on fire. Buck could eat jalapeno peppers and was no stranger to hot food, but this was liquid fire, molten lava.

He couldn't get his breath.

The owner saw what was happening and ran over. "Butter."

Buck couldn't focus on him as the man repeated, "Butter."

Finally, when he got no response, the restaurant owner grabbed the butter dish, got a healthy dollop of butter on two fingers and forced it into Buck's mouth.

The heat started to subside. Buck's eyes streamed tears.

He wiped them with his napkin and croaked, "Thanks."

The owner smiled. "Butter the only thing to quickly cut hot mustard. You never taste before?"

"No, and there's a second verse to that song. I won't ever be tasting it again. I take it that isn't a corn dog?"

"No," the owner laughed. "It an egg roll."

Duckworth's stomach was shaking, and his lips compressed trying not to laugh. "I tried to warn you."

Mrs. Simmons had the courtesy to mostly contain her laughter and was instead sympathetic to Buck's plight. Carol, on the other hand…well, Carol lost it entirely.

"I heard," Buck said, "but I heard too late."

"Apparently."

◊

They took Mrs. Simmons back to the office. On the way she said, "All of the files are still available to you if you need them."

Buck's face registered his surprise, and he turned in the seat to look at her. "I thought you sent them to us?"

"I sent you copies."

"You copied all those files?"

"As I said, I'm still being paid, I have to do something."

"We'll sure pay you for your time and the copy costs."

They pulled up in front of the office, and she got out. Before she closed the door, she said, "Mrs. Abernathy said it isn't necessary. She wants to do all she can to assist your investigation."

"I guess I should start by talking to her."

"That would be nice as a courtesy, but you will find she knew little if anything about the business. She really didn't want to know anything about his cases."

She went back into the office, and they drove over to Mrs. Abernathy's home in the Spring Branch area. Buck pulled out his handkerchief and blew his nose. "I still have this metallic feel or smell, or something, way up in my sinuses. Feels like it runs through my whole head."

"It'll pass in a couple of hours, Sheriff."

"If we're going to be spending this much time together you need to call me Buck."

"That doesn't feel right, but I'll try."

CHAPTER 9

Mrs. Abernathy's home was a nice three-bedroom brick on a lot totally shaded by large trees. The lawn was lush and green. When she came to the door, she turned out to be a slender woman with prematurely gray hair.

After brief introductions, she led them into her living room.

As they took seats, she said, "I hope Florence is being of assistance to you."

Buck was holding his hat in his hands, balancing it on his knee, he said, "More than I had any right to expect, but we don't wish to be a burden."

"Surely she told you that I put her and the office at your complete disposal. I want to aid your investigation all I can."

She told us that, and we really appreciate it, but we don't want to overdo it."

Her hands constantly moved as she talked. Small, delicate gestures that seemed to speak a language of their own. "You can't overdo it. Consider it *your* office and her your secretary while you are here. It makes me feel like I am helping out so the more you are able to utilize it the better, I feel about how much we are helping."

"What an amazing way to look at it. Thank you."

"Now, on to the case itself. I assume Florence told you that I know next to nothing about Delbert's cases or what he might be working on. He always felt he was working on the shady side of life and didn't want me exposed to it. I agreed with him, and apparently, it has turned out he was very right."

"Yes, she told us, and this is a courtesy call more than anything. I just wanted the chance to tell you how sorry I am, how sorry we all are for your loss."

The fluttering hands produced a handkerchief from somewhere, which she touched lightly to the corner of her eyes. "Thank you. I'm coming to terms with it, but it is hard. All these well-meaning people, but nothing they can say . . ."

"Yes ma'am, nobody can say anything that matters at a time like this. You know it, and they know it. But you just have to understand, they know you are hurting and want to help. They are offering to take a little part of your grief and carry it away. Look past the words to what they are offering and allow them to share it with you. The more of that grief you give away, the less you have."

She looked at him and smiled a small smile. "That's right, I had forgotten. You are a minister as well as a Sheriff, aren't you?"

"I am, and I have had a lot of experience with people experiencing grief."

"I've never looked at it quite that way, but I see what you are saying. You're right, the words really don't matter; it's the feelings that count."

"Yes, ma'am."

◊

They visited with her for about an hour, and other than giving an insight into his state of mind, she couldn't offer much. She did say he seemed very preoccupied before his last trip.

They rode in silence left for a good while after they before Duckworth said, "I have to say, Sheriff, what you told Mrs. Abernathy was nice. Very nice."

"I told the truth when I said I have to spend a lot of time with people that are grieving. I thought it was something she needed to hear."

Duckworth's eyes looked moist. "I lost my dad a few months ago, so your words kinda helped me, too. I just hadn't realized . . ."

Buck smiled and put a hand on the young deputy's shoulder. "I'm glad."

More time had passed in silence before Buck spoke up again. "We're going to the house of the woman with a cheating husband, right?"

"Yes, sir."

"The guy works for Oilfield Services?"

Carol looked at the file. "His name is Steve Sessions. Wife's name is Alice."

Buck turned to look at her. "All right, I doubt if he is going to be home since it's a work day, but we need to make sure before we get into it. The last thing I want to do is walk head-on into a domestic dispute with no warning. I don't mind counseling on them, but counseling and interrogating aren't the same thing. Besides, for all we know she might even be the woman in the car, and we have to be careful how we handle that, too."

They pulled up in front of the house. It was substantial and on a large lot.

Duckworth whistled softly. "You say this guy is a salesman? He must really sell a *lot*."

"Pretty much what I was thinking. We probably won't get into it here, but we may need to check with his company. I don't know what these guys make, but that's a lot of house."

When they rang the bell, a housekeeper answered the door. She asked them to wait, then returned shortly to ask them to follow her. Mrs. Sessions was sitting by the pool. She didn't look like she was casually sitting out, however; her hair was elaborately done, and she was wearing an expensive looking pant-suit. She looked more like she was on her way to the country club for lunch. She reeked of money.

Introductions were made, then she asked them to sit and asked if they would like a beverage of some sort. When they declined, she excused the housekeeper and watched her go back into the house before she turned and said, "You don't look like law enforcement people."

Buck pulled out the folding leather holder that had his badge on one side and his ID on the other. He had a friend over at the saddle shop make it in such a way that when he flipped it inside out, he could hang it on a shirt pocket to display his badge when needed. This time, he showed it and then put it away.

"Well, I suppose you are the real thing." She took a sip of her drink then looked up over the rim. "Am I in trouble?" she asked in a casual, almost flippant way.

"We just need to ask you a few questions. You are a client of a private investigator by the name of Abernathy."

She glanced quickly over her shoulder as if checking to see if her husband was there. Her whole demeanor changed. "How do you know that?"

"Abernathy has been killed. We found your name in his files."

"Killed? He's dead?"

"Yes, ma'am, murdered."

Her composure returned. "I guess that explains why I haven't had a report for a while. He was going out to a little town in West Texas where he expected to find something out."

"When was this?"

The dates she gave coincided with the time the victim was found. Buck jotted it down in his small pocket notebook. He saw Carol was taking notes as well, but he would rather have something twice than not get it at all.

"From the way you said that, it sounds like you didn't make the trip with him."

"*With him*? Why on earth would I do that?" She made it sound like such a trip was beneath her and the mere suggestion of it was offensive.

"We just have to try to make sure where everyone associated with the case was during that time period."

"You mean, do I have an alibi?"

"No, that would suggest we thought you were a suspect. Like I said, we're just trying to get everyone placed."

She wouldn't let go of it. "Are you saying you think my husband or the case have something to do with the murder? Or that I do?"

"No, like I said, just gathering information."

Her tone bordered on being snippy. "Well, I do have an alibi, whether you want to call it that or not. I was having some elective surgery done, and hospital records will account for the time nicely."

"Elective surgery?"

She sniffed. "If you can't tell what it was, then I may have wasted my money."

"It's not that, ma'am, just not up to me to say."

"Well, you can check with Memorial Hospital, and they should be able to satisfy your curiosity."

"I'm sure they will."

She got up. "If that is all, I have an appointment."

They got up. They were very aware they were being dismissed. "Thank you for seeing us."

Without a response, she walked back into the house and told the housekeeper to show them out.

On the way to the car, Carol said softly, "I think you got under her skin a bit."

Buck smirked, "Seemed that way, didn't it?"

Duckworth said, "Don't look now, but somebody is watching us from that upper window."

"You think it's her?"

"Could be, I can't see anything."

◊

As they drove over to the hospital, Carol said, "I think she's telling the truth. I don't think she's the woman in the car."

"Oh, really? And what do you base this on?"

"Just female logic I guess. It doesn't make sense to me that she would go with the PI to confront them until she knew what she was dealing with. She's a woman that would need to be in control of a situation. According to her statement and backed up by his file, she didn't know who the woman was, so it would make more sense to me for the woman in the car to be the woman her husband was involved with there in town."

"That does make sense to me, too," Buck said. "Wonder how we'd go about finding out who she is? Apparently, you are correct, Abernathy hadn't identified her, or it would be in the file."

Duckworth spoke up. "Or maybe he had found out and hadn't had time to put it in the file."

Buck stared at him. "Wonder why that hadn't occurred to me yet?"

At the hospital, patient confidentiality regulations were a problem. About all Buck was able to confirm was that she had elective surgery around that time, but specifics were not released.

"So she's off the hook?" Duckworth asked on the way to the car.

Buck grimaced. "It looks like she couldn't be the woman in the car. But does that mean she couldn't be involved? Let's think about it."

They got back to the car and got in before he continued. "If she isn't the woman in the car, and her husband was the driver, then likely Carol is right about who that woman is."

Carol smiled. "Literally the 'other woman,' pun intended."

"Exactly. But let's walk that further. What if her husband isn't the driver?"

"Then we don't know who the woman in the car is," Carol said, "not to mention who the driver is."

"Yes, we have to be careful making assumptions. Doing so

can blind us to other options that we may not have considered. We're putting a puzzle together, and the pieces that we've found fit but we can't tell anything about what the picture is going to be yet."

"We're here," Duckworth said.

Buck looked around. "We're where?"

"This is the office of Oilfield Services."

"Oh, yeah, I'm glad you're on top of things, I was completely distracted."

It was a three-story, brick building, but Buck didn't know how much of it was Oilfield Services. They made their way into the lobby where Buck flashed his badge and asked who was in charge. He was told the President was out of the office and asked if the office manager could help. He said he thought that would work.

A distinguished-looking older lady came across the lobby and offered her hand. "I'm Karen Burton. How may I be of assistance?"

"An employee of yours, Steve Sessions, is a person of interest in an investigation we're conducting. Can you answer a couple of questions for us?"

"If it was important enough to bring you all the way from West Texas, perhaps it shouldn't be discussed standing in the lobby. Will you follow me?"

She led them into a small conference room, and when they were seated, she said, "Are you free to tell me the subject of the investigation?"

"Not at this time, but since Mr. Sessions calls on your office there in Clear Creek, we believe he may know something that will help us."

"He isn't here at the present time; he's in the field."

"We'll catch up to him. We just came from talking with his wife. Can you confirm whether he was at that office June 18th through 20th?"

She picked up the phone on the table, made a brief call, and said, "Yes, we can confirm that he was there during that time period."

"Thank you. That's primarily what we needed." Buck hesitated. "I don't mean to get personal, and I confess I don't know whether it would play a role in our investigation or not, but something raised my curiosity about him."

"I'd be glad to help if I can."

"Well, to be blunt, it's his house ma'am. That's a mighty big house for someone on a salesman's salary."

She laughed. "You're exactly right. He's a good salesman, but he doesn't make that kind of money. We've talked about it here in the office, and we are given to understand that his wife came from money. She is supposed to be quite well off."

"After meeting her, I can certainly believe that," Buck said.

"Is there anything else?"

"No, ma'am, not unless you have something to add that might help us understand him a bit better."

"No, nothing I can say for a fact, and I don't want to gossip, but there is some office scuttlebutt that I suppose you should hear if it impacts your investigation." Her look suggested that she really didn't mind sharing a little gossip at all.

"Such as what?"

"It's a pretty strong rumor that he is cheating on his wife."

Well, well, I didn't even have to fish for it, she just dropped it right out there. "Really? If she is wealthy as you say, that doesn't sound very smart to me."

She sniffed. "That's the prevailing opinion, all right. And most feel if she can prove it, that she intends to divorce him and cut him off from her money entirely."

"That sounds like motive," he said softly.

"Motive for what?"

"I'm sorry, ma'am, I didn't realize I said that aloud. I shouldn't have. Let me just say that you've been very helpful."

On the way to the car, Buck said, "I didn't intend to say it out loud, but that certainly does sound like motive."

CHAPTER 10

Duckworth grinned at Buck. "So, Sheriff, are you going to want to take another try at Oriental food for dinner?"

Buck smiled. "Actually, I would like to try it again. I really couldn't even taste the food the first time after that hot mustard. But I think maybe not again quite so fast."

"How about some seafood, then? That's something I'm sure you don't get in West Texas."

"No, we're too far away from fresh seafood."

"I'm going to take you over to a place that not only has fresh seafood but has a lot of cooking with a Cajun touch."

"Cajun?" Not a term Buck was familiar with.

"It's a group of people that came from French-speaking Canada down to the Louisiana swamps and bayous. Very proud of their heritage and lifestyle. You find a lot of them that have made their way over into the gulf coast area. People are really fond of their cooking."

"I'd say that's something I've never had. How about you, Carol?"

"New to me, too."

Duckworth pulled into the parking lot at the restaurant. Buck said, "That's quite a name. How do you pronounce it?"

"Papadeaux. You pronounce it papa-dough."

"Okay, lead on Deputy."

It was a large dining room, very nicely appointed, with wait staff wearing crisp white jackets. They asked for and were given a quiet table in the corner. As they perused the menus, Buck perched his reading glasses on his nose, looked over at Duckworth and said, "You have some suggestions?"

"Oh, yeah, I'm going to start with some oysters on the half shell and a cup of seafood gumbo. Then I think I'm going to have the Jambalaya."

"What was that last one?"

"It's a shrimp, sausage and chicken dish in spicy Cajun seasonings. Very good, but it can be a little hot."

Buck made a sour face. "I think I've had enough hot for today."

Carol said, "If you get a dozen oysters, I'll split them with you."

"Sounds good. Buck, you want in on the oysters?"

Buck grimaced. "I think I'll pass on the oysters, too."

"At least try the gumbo," Duckworth said. "It has a dark rich roux and a lot of different kinds of seafood in it. It's not very spicy, and I think you'll like it."

All three opted for the gumbo, then Carol decided on a lobster, and Buck decided on the mixed seafood grill. They settled back to wait for their food.

"We made some progress today," Buck said. "Even if it doesn't feel like we are any closer to an answer."

Carol pulled out her notebook. "At this point, we have three possibilities. We've ruled out Mrs. Sessions as the woman in the car, but that doesn't mean her husband isn't involved."

"Agree, and we found what looks like a possible motive for

him."

"Yes, I have that. We also have the theft of the oilfield supplies, and right now, we're looking at Walker as a possibility on that. The third is the battle for control of the ranch, and we don't know much about that yet."

"Good summary. I'll call Helen in the morning, and we can go talk to her."

Their food came, and Duckworth did the honors of mixing the fresh horseradish into the cocktail sauce to the proper consistency. Then he and Carol made short work of the oysters before the arrival of the cups of gumbo. She gave Buck one last chance, "You sure you don't want to try one of these?"

He dismissed the idea with a simple shake of his head.

He did, however, greatly enjoy the gumbo. It was very thick and rich. "You were right about this stuff; it's good."

The main course arrived, and Buck eyed Carol's lobster. He shook his head. "I'll tell you, it was a really brave man that first looked at one of those things and said, 'I think I could eat that.'"

◊

Helen Silsbee invited them out to her son's house at ten the next morning. While they were driving, Buck turned to Carol. "You need to know before we get there, I haven't been saying much about it, but I have a long history with the Silsbee Family. Jiggs was one of my best friends, and I've known the kids since they were born. It'll probably affect this interview, but it won't affect the way I pursue any leads we might get."

"Thank you for letting me know; I'll try to be sensitive to

that."

When they got to the house and were seated in the living room, introductions were made. Helen was an attractive lady, brunette, close to sixty years old, but in spite of the expensive pantsuit she had on, Buck knew she had been born and raised on a ranch and was pure cowgirl at heart. Harold Silsbee was there as well when they arrived. He was a husky, middle-aged man with dark, almost swarthy features. Buck didn't know if that would cause her to speak less candidly than if it was just her. He resolved to simply let it develop how it wanted to develop.

Buck opened it up. "Helen, I'm sorry I haven't been in touch since the funeral."

She put a hand on his arm. "I'm afraid I didn't tell you after the services what a wonderful job you did conducting them."

"It's much more personal when you're talking about a good man and a good friend."

"Thank you, Buck, he thought a lot of you, too, as do I."

"Thank you. Happy as I am to see you, let be upfront with you as to why we had to come. We had a private investigator turn up dead there in Clear Creek, and when we were going through his files looking for any local connections, your name turned up. We're following up on his files that have a local connection."

He glanced nervously at her son. Was he opening up something she didn't want him to hear?

She saw the look he gave her son and put him at ease. "It's all right, Buck, Harold knows all about me hiring Mr. Abernathy."

Buck couldn't seem to sit still. He got up and stood by the fireplace. "The file didn't shed much light on what he was doing for you. It just indicated he was looking into activities at the ranch."

"It was just business. None of the family lives on the ranch right now, and we wanted an independent look into how the Foreman was handling the place. We wanted to know if everything was on the up and up, the bills being paid, the stock all there, that sort of thing."

"It sounds more like you just needed an audit."

"Mr. Abernathy saw to that, too. You see, Buck, you've known my three boys and our girl all their lives, but what you probably don't know is they are all at odds over the ranch. Some want to sell it and divide the money, one wants to go back and run it, but others are blocking him because they don't trust him to do it. It's a mess."

"Talking about inheritances can cause friction in the best of families. Did Abernathy find anything out?"

"Not conclusively. He was still looking into it, but he had found some irregularities he was looking into further."

"Irregularities?" Buck sat back down across from her, perched on the edge of his chair. "How serious?"

"I'd say very serious—missing money, missing cattle—but he hasn't come forward with proof."

He sat back, frowning. "Helen, this is criminal activity. You should have reported it to me."

"It's not that easy, Buck."

"Why not?"

"Because it may be family."

Harold stopped being a silent observer. "My brother, Jack,

would do anything to get control of the ranch, Sheriff...anything."

Buck mulled that situation over. Jack had always been Jiggs and Helen's cross to bear. A headstrong boy, he had always pushed his limits.

After their meeting, Helen walked them to the door. Then she pulled Buck aside and asked if he would mediate a meeting between her and her kids back at the ranch. She said she hoped, as the Sheriff, he could get to the bottom of what was going on at the ranch, and, as a minister, he could do the counseling necessary to help put her family back together again. He agreed to do it, and she said she would make the arrangements.

◊

They pulled back into the parking lot of the PI's office and went in. Mrs. Simmons looked up and gave them a bright smile. "You make any progress?"

Buck returned her smile with something more like a grimace. "I'm not sure we learned anything that helps. Instead of answers, I think we just got more questions."

She nodded. "Delbert used to say that a lot."

"Delbert? Oh, yeah, Abernathy. I guess we haven't used his first name a lot."

"I understand. If there were clients in here, I'd call him Mr. Abernathy."

"One interesting development; after our meeting, Mrs. Silsbee asked me if I'd mediate a meeting between her and her kids back at the ranch. She said she hoped maybe I could do the counseling necessary to help put her family back together again. I agreed to do it, and she's making the arrangements."

"Sounds like they are having family problems," Carol said.

"It does, doesn't it?"

Mrs. Simmons changed the subject. "I've been spending a lot of time going through files. I guess I'm hoping I would spot something that you wouldn't see. You know, being familiar with things and all."

"You having any luck?"

"The three you've singled out all seem to have ties to the oilfield. Oilfield theft, a salesman in the oil field, and according to the file, part of the problem at the ranch is squabbling over some potential oil exploration."

"I think that's why the family is fighting over it. I think it's more about oil than it is ranching."

"I thought that too," she agreed. "I've been looking in other files that don't have an apparent connection to your town but do have an oilfield connection."

"You know, there might be a real future for you as an investigator."

She laughed. "Maybe in someone else's office; I don't see me out doing the legwork. Anyway, this file interested me." She handed a file folder to Buck. "Like I say, I can't make a connection in it to Clear Creek, but there does seem to be a lot of interest in it on a person named Jack Silsbee."

Buck glanced up. "You don't say? Who's the client?"

"That's just it, there isn't a client. It seems to be just something he was looking into himself."

"Not for Mrs. Silsbee?"

"I don't see where he has talked to her about it, or it would have been in her file. He seems to have been keeping it separate for a reason."

"Well now, that is interesting."

◊

Deputy Duckworth took them back to the airport and stopped at their airline terminal. He was in a regular patrol car and back in uniform. Buck offered his hand and said, "You've been a big help."

"I've enjoyed it, Sheriff. First time I've felt like an investigator instead of a traffic cop."

"Son, most of law enforcement is just doing the job each day. I don't do investigating on a daily basis either. It's mostly just dealing with people and their problems. Trying to keep them safe."

"Seems like in a big city like this, the contacts are all negative. I don't get to deal with people much unless there's trouble…or unless they're speeding, and they aren't too happy when I deal with them about that."

"I suppose there is an advantage to being in a small town; we deal with people on a more personal basis."

"Maybe I would be a better fit in a small town."

Buck laughed. "Well, you've got a job if you ever want it. I'd hate for Sheriff Everly to think I was stealing his people, though."

"Oh, if I ever decide to come talk to you about it, I'd take care of that. I would kinda like to stay in touch with this case, though."

"You might stay in touch with Mrs. Simmons. I expect she's going to be in the loop until we're through with this."

CHAPTER 11

Buck got back from the airport to find Doc, Barney, and Raul on his porch. As Buck got out of the car, Raul said, "Good trip?"

"Not bad if you mean from a travel standpoint. If you mean progress on the case, I think I'm coming back with more questions than answers."

"Too bad."

Doc said, "I take it you dropped Carol off?"

"She wanted some time to decompress."

Doc looked over his glasses at him. "How was it traveling with her?"

"Great. There's more to her than her reserved, Marine-corps-trained exterior."

"What does that mean?"

"It means she was a good traveling companion, and it afforded me the chance to be invisible."

"Invisible?" Barney didn't get that one.

"Barney, I don't know why I never noticed it before, I guess because she's always so squared away and professional, but Carol is a beautiful woman."

Raul snorted soft drink out his nose. "You just now figuring that out?"

"In soft clothes and her hair down, it's pretty hard to ignore. Guys, I could have been walking around buck naked, and nobody would have noticed for looking at her."

Barney grinned. "Buck naked—now there's a play on words."

"You know what I mean."

"It works either way."

"As much as I'm enjoying hearing about your budding romance," Doc said. "I'd like to hear what you found out about the case."

Buck flushed red in his cheeks and neck. "Romance—Doc, you know better than that. Why Carol is—"

They laughed. "I know," Doc said, "like a daughter to you."

"A daughter? I don't know that I'd say that but . . ."

Barney said, "Don't worry, Buck, nobody figures you have anything going with Carol."

Now Buck looked offended. "Are you saying you think I'm too old?"

Doc snorted. "Hey, you're the one who said you were getting so old that you hadn't even noticed how pretty she was."

"I guess you've got me there."

Raul tried to help out. "The case?"

Buck looked grateful to change the subject. "We went there with three suspects, and we came back with three suspects. We gathered some information, but we haven't cleared anybody."

"I knew there were three leads," Raul said. "I hadn't heard three suspects."

"One of the sons from the Silsbee ranch may be a person of interest now. Whatever is going on, it seems to be pretty oilfield related. But did anything happen while I was gone?"

Raul smiled. "Yeah, you'll love this. We had an attempted

robbery out at the Deli-Mart."

"Attempted?"

"A kid came in with a black ski mask on and a small caliber handgun and stuck the gun in Bert's face."

"Knowing Bert, I'm guessing he did not take it well."

"That's putting it mildly. He jerked a double barrel coach shotgun from under the counter and stuck right back it in the kids face."

Buck whistled. "That's an attention getter."

"He said, 'Let's just shoot each other. I was shot three times while I was in the service, and they used guns bigger than that pea-shooter you have; I'm still here. You aren't going to like being shot by this shotgun, though. Good thing I have that video camera to identify you, because you aren't going to have enough head left to recognize.'"

"That should have done it."

"It did. The kid dropped the gun into the puddle of urine at his feet."

Buck laughed until he had tears in his eyes. Finally, gasping for breath, he said, "I reckon I would have wet myself, too, looking down the barrel of that thing."

Raul nodded. "Word of this gets around, and I don't think anybody is going to try Bert again...ever."

◊

When Buck got into the office, he went up to the jail before getting started for the day. When the jailer greeted him, he asked where the kid was that tried to rob the Deli-Mart. The jailer pointed him to a cell.

The youth was sitting on the cot leaning against the wall in the corner. He looked sullen and depressed.

Buck motioned for the jailer to open the cell, and he took a seat on the empty cot across from the boy. "Reckon I'd be kinda down, too, if I'd gone through what just happened to you."

The kid scooted to the edge of the cot. "That guy out at that store is crazy. I think he would really have shot me."

"You can bet the farm he would have shot you. He shot people while he was in the army, he knows how. You will never come closer to dying than you did right then."

"I believe it. The barrels on that shotgun looked as big as railroad tunnels."

"I'm sure they did," Buck agreed. "I looked at your record. You've never had a brush with the law before. Why now?"

The boy looked downcast. "I have a wife, a new baby, and no job. The kid's gotta have formula."

"If you'd have walked in and told Bert that, he'd have just given you the money for it."

"You think so?"

"I know so. I'll tell you what, I'll go over and speak for you when you come before the judge. With no record, I think we can get you probation. But I don't think you're cut out for a life of crime."

"No, sir, I have to agree with you on that. I just couldn't think of anything else to do. I can't find a job."

Buck got up. "For now, I'll send a deputy out with some formula and some groceries from our church benevolence fund.

After we get you clear with the judge, we'll see what we can do."

The boy got up and shook his hand. "I don't know how to thank you, sir."

"You can thank me by asking for help when you need it instead of trying to take it yourself."

"I've learned my lesson, believe me."

"I do believe you, son. I do believe you."

Buck went down to his office, sat down in his chair and looked up the number for the Deli-Mart. "Hello, Bert?"

"Oh, hello, Buck."

"Listen, I just talked to the kid that tried to rob you. Turns out he was trying to get money for baby formula..."

Buck thought he could have heard Bert even without the phone. "For Baby formula? He shoulda just told me what his problem was."

"Yeah, I told him if he'd just asked you..."

"What's going to happen to him? He have a record?"

"No, he has no record, and will probably get probation..."

"I feel kinda bad about it all now. Would it help if I was there when he goes before the judge? I could speak up for him."

"Yes, I think it would help if you were there to speak for him. I'll tell you when."

"Maybe if I told the judge I was giving him a job it would help."

"Oh, yeah, if you gave him a job that would help things a lot...You're a good man, Bert."

As he hung up, Raul and Carol came into Buck's office, ever-present cups of coffee in their hands. "You get the kid straightened out?" Raul said.

"How'd you know I talked to the kid?"

Raul eased his big frame into the chair across from the desk as Carol took the other one. "You come in and go straight to the jail? Doesn't take much to figure that."

"I think he'll get probation. Bert is going to give him a job."

"That's good. I expect he'll toe the line as long as he knows that shotgun is there."

"I don't think a threat is necessary. I think the boy has seen the light. Now to business, we have to get back on this case. We need to figure out what our next step is."

"I was pretty busy while you two were gone, but when I could, I spent more time looking through files."

"Mrs. Simmons found another one that might have a bearing."

"The one that mentions Jack Silsbee?"

"That's the one. You found it too, huh?"

"I did. I figure that's what you meant last night when you said another person of interest had surfaced."

"It is," Buck said. "I'm glad you didn't bring it up then."

"Didn't figure it was the right time."

"Well, Mrs. Silsbee has all her family coming in to the ranch Saturday. I'm supposed to be there to see about doing some so-called family counseling."

"And investigating?"

"Absolutely some investigating."

CHAPTER 12

The Silsbee ranch was not a large ranch by Texas standards, and though it stayed in the black, was not a major money producer. When "Jiggs" Silsbee was alive, he would never entertain any idea of selling the place and felt like he was leaving it as a legacy to his kids. His wife still felt that way, but the kids? Buck wasn't so sure.

They were all seated in the great room in front of the big rock fireplace that featured a full body mounting of a cougar lying on the mantle. Every time Buck saw the animal, he felt he knew exactly what the last thing was that the cat had thought. He could just hear it saying, "Oh, crap, is that a gun?"

One thing was for sure, it wouldn't kill any more Silsbee calves.

This was practically a second home for Buck. Jiggs had been his best friend, and he had known the kids from the day they were born. It made this investigation that much harder. When talking about the investigation with others he made sure to downplay the very close relationship that was there, but that relationship was going to make this meeting hard.

Harold and Jack both took after their dad, dark features that appeared even darker with the jet-black hair. The third brother, Jimmy, and his sister, Linda, both took after their mother. They were light-haired and easy going.

Helen looked different on the ranch. In town, she had been

impeccably dressed and an absolute lady, yet to Buck, seemed to have the attitude of a fish out of water. Here in comfortable surroundings and dressed in a plaid shirt and jeans, she looked more at home. Buck knew without hearing it that she would rather be living here.

She looked at her assembled brood and said, "As I told you, I've asked Buck to help us sort through things. I know you all know he was one of your father's closest friends, and in addition to being the Sheriff, he is a minister and well-suited to counsel families in time of grief."

Jack glowered. "And I told you it wasn't necessary for him to be here. This is family business, and he has no place here."

"I asked him, and he stays. You boys are too headstrong for me. Jiggs could handle you, but you just run rough-shod over me."

"Not all of us," Jimmy and Linda said in unison.

She squeezed Jimmy's hand, "No, not all of you."

Buck said, "I know you two boys resent me being here, but you have no choice. The will clearly leaves everything to your mother, and it's up to her to decide what your position is in this ranch and this estate. She isn't comfortable doing it without a little help, and I plan to give her that help. You had best cooperate, or you won't like the advice I might give her."

She said very softly, "Thank you, Buck, and just so they know, I trust you completely and will be inclined to take whatever action you might suggest."

Jack bristled. "I for one don't like it."

Harold seemed to read the writing on the wall. "I'm not fond of the idea either, but I'll go along with it. I know Dad trusted you,

Buck."

The lines were drawn; the stage was set. Buck said, "Okay, let's get to it. It would help me to understand if each of you shares what you feel needs to be done. No arguing, no hassle, just what you would like to see happen. Harold, suppose you go first."

Harold shrugged. "Everybody knows how I stand."

"I don't, so humor me."

"I think the ranch should be sold and the money distributed equally between us. I could take that lump sum, invest it and make it grow. If she wanted, I could handle mother's money and grow hers as well. Of course, she is more than welcome to continue staying with me as long as she wants."

"Jack, what are your thoughts?"

"I think the ranch should be kept, but ranching operations should cease. This thing is break-even at best. But there is oil under this place, and I think we need to start going after it. Oil is where the money is. We could sell off the physical plant, house, barn, equipment, livestock and all that and split that money. And I, for sure, don't want Harold handling any of my money for me. I could do more with mother's money, as well, investing it in oil wells."

Harold scoffed, "The way you have yours, I suppose?"

"I've made millions in oil."

"And turned right around and lost them again on the next dry hole."

"Just because I've had a couple of bad breaks . . ."

Buck interceded. "I said there would be no arguing on this, people are just making their case at this point. Linda, I believe you are the next oldest. What would you like to see?"

"Daddy loved this place and would never stand still to see all or any of it sold. I don't want to see it sold either. Harold and Jack just won't take time to listen to mother, but she loves it here, too. She was right, they just run over her."

"But what do *you* want to see?"

"I'd like to see the ranch continue. I'd love to live here myself, but I have my own family, and I have to live where my husband's job is. I do love having it for us to come to when we can. I guess I'm being selfish, but that's how I feel."

Harold and Jack both started to say something, but Buck raised a hand to shut them off. "Jimmy, it's your turn."

He smiled brightly. "I love this place. It's home. I finish college in May with a degree in ranch management. I always thought I would come run the place, but my brothers have no confidence in me. I could make it pay, and mother would always have a home here, and Linda and the rest of the family would always have a place to come."

"Your father was so happy you were studying on how to improve the place," Helen said. "He was eager for you to come back and try."

"To eke out a living instead of making real money," Jack said.

"It'd produce more selling it and investing," Harold said.

Buck barked, "Stop it! You guys just can't keep from arguing, can you? Helen, the last say is yours."

She started to speak with her head down, her voice barely a whisper. Buck stopped her and moved between her and the boys. He sat down on the coffee table with his back to them and took both of her hands in his own. From this position, she couldn't see anyone but him. "You aren't talking to them, Helen, you're talking to me. I don't want to hear what you think is good for the family. I don't want to hear what you think will make the most money. I want to know what *you* want."

She looked up, tears in her eyes. Softly she said, "I want to come home."

Jack erupted, "I knew this would happen if we got some preacher involved! We had her thinking right, and now he's got her all mixed up again."

Buck spun on him. He was shorter by a head, but he advanced on him, poking him in the chest with a finger, backing him up as he spoke. "Got her thinking right? You mean you managed to bully her into your way of thinking. The only problem is you two idiots can't agree on what you're trying to bully her into. You aren't thinking of her; you're only thinking of yourselves."

He spun on Harold. "And you're playing the good son, letting her live with you. You're only doing that to keep her under your thumb so you can work on her to accept your ideas for the place. I figure once you got control of her part of the money, she'd be in a nursing home in a heartbeat."

"I'd never do that."

"So you say. Well here's a little surprise for you. You guys are working so hard trying to browbeat and bully her, and she doesn't even have a say in what is going to happen."

"*What?*" they yelled in unison.

"She signed a power of attorney giving me the right to decide what happens. She knows I will do what is best for her, not you."

The two boys started screaming at him, while Linda and Jimmy went to their mother to tell her she had done the right thing.

"This isn't right," Jack said. "You're trying to weasel us out of our money."

"You may be right the way you're acting now, but you can be sure I'll never take a penny of it for myself. Okay, for the time being, here's what's going to happen. Helen, you are home starting right now. Harold, anything she left at your place will be shipped back within the next few days. You got that?"

"You have no right to do this!"

"You want to take a chance on getting cut out of this, too? Jack seems dead set on accomplishing it. I asked if you got what I told you to do."

Harold had a sullen look on his face, but he nodded.

"Linda, you and Jimmy are welcome to stay with her the remainder of the weekend. Matter of fact, I'd love to see all three of you at church tomorrow." He turned on the other two boys. "You two are leaving. I don't like the frame of mind that you are in, and I don't want you working on her to change the power of attorney. You see, we figured you would do that, and there is a codicil in it that doesn't allow it to be overturned without the consent of the district judge, and he is well-apprised of the situation. He will not let you intimidate her. I'll stay here until you two boys are gone."

They spun on their heels and walked out, grumbling. Jack grabbed a ladder-back chair as he passed it and threw it across the room.

Buck went out on the porch to watch them drive off. Helen

came up beside him. He turned to her. "I know that wasn't easy for you. I hope before this is all over that we'll be able to repair that relationship, but for now, a clean break was required."

She looked up at him with tears in her eyes. "I hope you're right. It feels so awful."

◊

Harold and Jack went into a bar at the airport. Harold said, "I sure didn't see this coming."

"Neither did I," Jack agreed. "We've got to quit fighting each other on this. We need to pool our resources. We need a lawyer, and a good one."

They got their drinks and moved over to a small table in the corner. "He said the power of attorney can't be broken," Harold said. "But any legal action can be reversed. To do so will be expensive."

"I've got some money I can put into it."

Harold looked surprised. "Where'd you get money?"

"I have my ways."

"We've got some high-powered lawyers in Houston; I'll look into it."

"Yeah," Jack whispered, looking around, "and don't forget, if the Sheriff ain't around, then neither is that power of attorney."

Harold looked shocked. "What are you saying?"

"I'm saying all problems can be solved."

"I don't want to be any party to something like that."

"I didn't say I was going to do anything. He's an old man, things could change."

CHAPTER 13

"Heard you had quite a party out at the Silsbee ranch." Doc cradled a soft drink can on his belly as they sat on the porch.

"Those older boys are a piece of work," Buck agreed.

Barney said, "I don't think you've heard the last of them."

"No, I don't expect I have. As long as they come after me and not their mother…"

"I don't envy you being in the middle," Doc said. "I know how you feel about that family."

"We do go way back. You know, it's funny, but they always struck me as an unlikely pair, her and Jiggs. She's so quiet and reserved, and Jiggs was so brash and bull-headed."

"Good-hearted, though," Doc said. "He'd give you his last dime."

Buck nodded. "Yep, he was a good man, the best. Boys got his brashness, but they missed out on the good-hearted part."

Doc said, "Shame they didn't take after their mother."

"Two of them did—the girl and the youngest boy. Good kids."

"I'm thinking they'll lawyer-up now," Barney returned to the subject.

"Yeah, I think that's next. But Judge Tolliver is briefed on it; I don't think he'll go for it."

"They'll try for a change of venue," Barney said.

"He can handle that, too. I don't believe he will allow her to be intimidated."

"They have to be pretty mad at you."

"That's an understatement. I think if I work it right, Harold might eventually come around. Jack I'm not so sure about, but we're looking at him closer anyway."

"In connection to what?"

"Too early to say, Barney. Just looking."

◊

Shortly after Buck got to his office, he sent upstairs to have Roger brought down. He looked up when the man appeared in his door and said, "You sent for me, Sheriff?"

"I could have come up there to talk to you, but I thought you'd like to get out for a while."

This wasn't the belligerent man Buck had put behind bars. He was somehow different. "I do get out for exercise every day, but you're right, this is different. This feels almost...well...normal."

Raul came in and brought Roger a cup of coffee. "They treating you all right up there?"

"Good as anybody might expect being behind bars. I know I asked for it. I'm doing my time."

Raul gave him a pat on the shoulder and went back out.

Buck studied him as he took a tentative sip. "You don't seem to be thinking you got a raw deal anymore."

The look he gave Buck seemed to imply sincerity. "Being behind bars while you're cold sober gives a man time to think."

"Have you been reading that New Testament I gave you?"

"I have. And it makes a lot of sense. But there's an awful lot I don't understand."

"They call it a great mystery, and it is. You see, salvation is a gift, but one that has to be accepted on faith, not on understanding." Buck came around and sat on the edge of the desk in front of Roger. "We aren't supposed to understand without God's help. Once we commit to Jesus and get saved, that is a great gift, but we are given another gift. We receive the help of the Holy Spirit, and that help allows us to decipher and understand what we read. But we have to start by simply accepting in faith."

"I think I get that. When I get out, I'll come to your church and . . ."

"You don't have to wait. If you're ready, we can pray the sinner's prayer right here."

"I think I *am* ready."

◊

Raul stuck his head in the door. "I saw you guys down on your knees; was that what I think it was?"

"It was me leading Roger in the sinner's prayer. He got saved."

"That's great news. Maybe he'll turn his life around now."

"He's made a good start. He not only got saved, but he's trying to come clean as well."

"How so?"

"He wanted to know if I could get him a deal if he solved the oilfield thefts for me. I told him I would if he would agree to testify, and he said he would. I called the judge, and he agreed."

"What'd he give you?"

"What I expected. He said he opened the gate for the thefts, but that it was Jack Silsbee and some men who actually did it."

"Well now, we thought those might be connected in some way."

"So Roger is no longer a suspect?"

"I didn't say that. We only have his word on it, and he could be simply trying to deflect suspicion onto someone else. But the oilfield thefts might just be the tip of the iceberg. Abernathy was investigating these thefts. That would give Silsbee an awful strong motive for killing him."

Raul whistled. "That makes sense. How do we prove it?"

"That's a good question."

"So we go arrest him now?"

"I think it might be a good idea to let it play out a little more. We've got him on the theft, and we have the witness safely on ice assuming his testimony was true and would stand up. I'd rather see if he's the one who killed Abernathy and tie that to him."

"So it's the proverbial 'give him some rope'?"

"Let's see what he does with it."

◊

Buck drove out to the Silsbee ranch. Helen met him on the porch.

He removed his hat. "Morning, Helen, you look so much more relaxed."

"I am, thanks to you. It's so good to be home. And it's so good not having the boys leaning on me all the time about what they want me to do."

"Hopefully, we've put a stop to that. Would you like to go over here and sit down?"

They walked over to a couple of chairs and sat. "Have you heard from them since they left?"

"Not from Jack. Harold called to say he wanted to apologize for being difficult at the meeting and that he has sent my belongings to me."

"That's good. There may be hope for him yet. I'm thinking when I get a plan developed for the ranch that we may have need of his investment abilities. That may placate him considerably."

"How about Jack?"

"There are some oilfield-related things that may involve him all right." *That's the honest truth; no need to know they aren't good things. Not yet.*

A car entered the ranch gate and headed for the house. She looked surprised, "Why, that's Jimmy's car."

"Yes, I asked him to meet us here."

He rushed up on the porch and hugged his mother. "Hi, mom. Hello, Sheriff."

"Hello, Jimmy. Thanks for coming."

He pulled up a chair to form a tight little circle. "So, why did you want to see me?"

"Straight to the point, I like that," Buck said. "All right, I have in mind developing a plan for what to do with the ranch, but since that is what you are studying to do, I want you to do most of it."

"Me?" Jimmy was clearly surprised.

"Who better to write a business plan for a ranch than someone studying ranch management?"

"I can do that," he grinned. "I really can."

"I need you to research it and write it as if you were going to submit it to the bank if you were trying to get funding for a brand new operation."

His enthusiasm was infectious. "Some of my professors would even help."

"There are certain variables I'd like you to address in it."

"Give me a minute." He went into the house and came back with a pen and paper. "Okay, shoot."

"Variable number one, you do have access to an expert investment advisor with a vested interest in the ranch."

"You're talking about Harold."

"I am. Factor him in. Second, Jack is probably correct, there are probably some possibilities for oil development, but they do not have to preclude the successful operation of the ranch. I want you to propose a way to do that."

"With a role for Jack, I take it?"

"That would be fine, although that situation may change. Now, the biggest part of it, I need a plan to put the ranching operation on a successful footing. I propose the plan assumes you will be managing the ranch for the family, but you will also need a good foreman. I suggest you talk to the current foreman to see if you feel you two can work together."

Jimmy was clearly surprised. "You want *me* to manage it?"

"Don't you think you can?"

"Of course, I do, but my brothers don't."

"Your brothers aren't calling the shots here. Your father expected you to be able to come back and do it; I know your mother believes in you, and I have confidence in you."

Jimmy seemed to grow several inches right in front of their eyes. "Is that all?"

"No, there will be much more—inventory of the livestock, looking over needed physical changes, a thorough examination of the books and accounts—but that's what you've been studying, right?"

"Right. I can work all that up."

"I need it as quickly as you can get it done."

CHAPTER 14

Buck's phone was ringing as he walked back into his office. He crossed the room and answered it. "Sheriff Green."

"Sheriff, this is Harold Silsbee."

"Hello, Harold, what can I do for you?"

"It's more what I can do for you, Sheriff. But first, let me apologize for the way I acted when we were at the house."

"Your mother has already told me you said that."

"Well, I meant it. I've been so focused on trying to get mother to do what I thought was the right thing that I didn't even realize what might be best for her. Not until you slapped me across the face with it like a wet fish. Even then, my first reaction was to get defensive. But I really do want you to believe I would have *never* taken her money and stuck her in a nursing home. I hope you believe that."

"I do believe it, Harold. Your mother was really upset after I threw you boys out, but I told her a little shock value was what was needed."

"It got to me. But I don't think it got to Jack. I wanted you to know that Jack and I have talked about getting together and hiring a good lawyer to try and break that power of attorney."

"I expected that. I don't believe it will be successful, but I did figure that would be your next move."

"I haven't done it yet, and I'm not sure it's the right move. But that's not the reason I called. It's been weighing on me. When we were talking about our next move, he made a statement I can't forget. He said, 'If the Sheriff ain't around, then neither is that power of attorney.' And I believe he meant it."

"You think he intends to try and kill me?" Buck sat down in his chair.

"That or hire it done."

Buck rubbed the back of his neck. "And you think he is capable of it?"

"Sheriff, I think he is capable of anything to get what he wants."

Buck leaned forward and lowered his voice. "Can you keep a confidence?"

"I can."

"We have a witness that can send your brother to jail for the theft of thousands of dollars in oilfield supplies."

"He did say he had a way of getting his money for the lawyer. Why haven't you arrested him?"

"If he is willing to try to kill me, he may be involved in the death of another person."

"You're talking about that private investigator."

"I am."

"I wouldn't want to think that of him but, to be honest, I couldn't put it past him. Sheriff, he's my brother, and I love him, but he's gone more and more off the deep end over the past few years. Like I said, these days, I think he's capable of anything."

"If you could help, would you do it?"

"I don't want to, but you say he's going to jail anyway?"

"Without a doubt."

"I couldn't live with it if I did nothing, and you were killed, and maybe I'll even be helping him if I can keep him from doing something worse. I'll do whatever you need."

"If you told him you were on board with getting rid of me, and we put a wire on you, do you think you could get him to talk?"

"With his ego? No problem."

"You'd have to be able to sell it."

"I was a pretty good actor in school plays in high school."

"You'd need to question his ability to get it done. Maybe he'd admit he had done it before."

"I think I can pull that off."

◊

"So, two of our leads have merged into one?" Carol came into Buck's office.

"I wouldn't say that. If this was a horse race, I'd say one lead has pulled out in front, but we have no corroboration on Walker other than his word. The preacher in me tends to believe him, to take him at his word, but the lawman keeps saying proof, we have to have proof."

"So I take it we don't forget the third one, the cheating husband?"

"We can't afford to forget any leads. I'll admit Silsbee is looking pretty good for it, but until we know for sure, we have to keep digging."

"I get it," Carol said.

But for now, I guess I'd better call the Sheriff in Harris

County and see if I can set this sting operation up on Jack Silsbee." He placed the call and asked to speak to Sheriff Everly.

"Jerry, this is Buck Green."

"Hello, Buck, what can I do for you?"

"I hate to impose on you a second time, but you could save me a trip down there if you were a mind to."

"Happy to help, Buck. What is it this time?"

"I need a wire on a man who is trying to get his brother to confess to a crime. He knows what to say, all I need is for somebody to set it up and do the recording. In fact, your man Duckworth has a real interest in the case since he helped us on it. Do you suppose it is something he could do?"

"Yes, I think he could handle it."

"If we get something on him, I would appreciate it if you'd arrest him and hold him; I can send a deputy to pick him up."

"How about if we score on it, we just arrest him and I'll have Duckworth transport him. You'll need to reimburse the travel expenses of course."

"You sure you want to do that?" Buck said. "When we left, he was thinking maybe he belonged in a smaller department. If he came here, you might not get him back."

"He's a good man, but truthfully he may be a little naïve about law enforcement in the big city. He might be better off in a small town. I think it might be better for both departments if he got a look at it to see."

"You might be right. Just so you know, we already have the subject cold on another charge but need to find out about an additional charge. The man's name that you will be putting the wire on is Harold Silsbee. I'll have him call you, and I really appreciate it."

They said goodbye, and he hung up the phone. Carol was smiling. "So Duckworth may be transporting the prisoner?"

"It looks like it."

"That's nice."

Nice? Buck watched her walk away. *Interesting. Was there a little something going on here?* He might be on the verge of getting a new deputy.

◊

Now that he knew Jack was getting arrested one way or the other, he didn't want to spring it on Helen without her being prepared. He made the drive out to the ranch and found her in the kitchen. She poured them a cup of coffee, and they sat down at the table.

"Helen, I have some bad news for you. I wanted you to be prepared for it."

She looked sad. "And things were going so well." She sighed deeply, clasped her hands together in her lap, composed herself and said, "All right, what is it?"

"It's Jack."

She caught her breath. "Is he..."

"No, nothing like that. Helen, we have the evidence we need to put him away for grand theft."

She couldn't meet his eyes. "I knew it was something like that. He always has so much money, but he never seems to work."

"That's not all of it."

"Oh, dear."

"Harold called me. He thinks Jack is going to arrange to have me killed to get me out of the way."

She began to cry softly. "He couldn't do that…not that."

"Harold thinks he's serious. He's going to try to get him to confess on tape so he doesn't go to jail for something more serious than what he's already on the hook for."

Still sobbing she looked up at him. "Where did we go so terribly wrong?"

He moved over to take her hand. "Don't think like that. We can't live our children's life for them; we can only raise them the best we can and trust them to take it from there. No matter how good the up-raising, some just take a wrong path. Greed is usually behind it."

"I suppose so."

"I'm trusting you to not warn him. Harold is doing the right thing keeping him from doing something worse. You wouldn't be doing him any favors to warn him."

"No. No, I won't warn him. I do see this needs to be done."

CHAPTER 15

The stage was set at Harold's house. Duckworth set up in the bedroom upstairs, and wireless mikes were set up in the living room and one on Harold himself. They were taking no chances on getting a good recording.

Jack got to the house mid-morning. "Good idea to get together; we need to talk a little strategy on this."

They moved into the living room, and Harold fixed them a drink. "I agree we need to talk about it."

Jack held his glass up in a salute then took a sip. "There's enough in this for both of us."

"We have a mother and two siblings to think of as well."

"The way I figure it, it's every man for himself."

That grated on Harold. *How could my brother change so much that he no longer cares about his siblings or even his mother?* But he knew he had to act out his role. "I'm starting to think that way myself."

Jack took a long pull on his drink. "I thought you'd come around. Dad taught us to be tough. Taught us to take care of ourselves."

Dad was honest as the day was long. He'd be so ashamed of the way you are now. "I haven't gotten a lawyer yet. A high-profile lawyer costs more than I can handle; I think more than both of us can handle."

"I told you there's an easier way."

"That's hard for me to think about."

"You never were as strong as I am."

Maybe physically, but I've always been more responsible. But aloud he said, "That's true."

How to broach this so it doesn't sound like a trap? "If we were to get rid of that sheriff, how would we go about it?"

"I don't know about you, but I'm not about to do something like that myself. But this is a big city; there has to be somebody here that'd do it for money?"

"You don't know of someone?"

"Why would I know of someone? What do you think about me?"

"I know about the oil equipment thefts, I thought maybe you had something to do with getting rid of that private investigator since you seemed ready to do the same to Buck."

"Private investigator? He had nothing on me. Why would I risk a murder rap on something like that? But millions of dollars' worth of oil, that's different."

So he didn't kill that private investigator. I'm really glad. But he seems to be ready enough to kill now. I have to get him to say something so I can stop it. "So tell me what to do."

"We have to find somebody who will do it for us. Maybe if I go down to the lower east side and hit a few bars, I can find somebody. It's not like we can put an ad in the paper, you know."

"You're sure you want to go this route?"

"We don't have any choice. That sheriff is going to be a pain in the side from now on if we don't."

"I think that's enough, Harold." They turned to see the deputy standing in the doorway, pistol in hand. "Mr. Silsbee, I'm going to need you to get down on your knees with your hands on top of your head."

Jack spun on his brother. "You set me up? How could you do that to your own brother?"

He took a step toward him, but Duckworth jacked the action on his pistol and said, "I wouldn't do that. I told you to get on your knees, hands clasped on your head, and I mean right now."

Jack did as he was told. Duckworth came around and fastened one cuff of the handcuffs on his left wrist. He pulled his hands back behind him, then finished cuffing him. Once his hands were secured, the deputy patted him down but found no weapons.

Jack looked at his brother with hate in his eyes. "I'll get you for this. I trusted you."

"Someday, you'll realize I kept you from doing something much worse than you have already done."

"That's another thing. I'm dumb as dog food. It just dawned on me. Why didn't I ask you how you knew about the drill pipe thefts? That should have been a tip-off, but I just wasn't thinking."

"Okay, you two. That's enough talk. We've got a trip to make."

◊

Buck walked up on the porch. Doc and Barney were always there, permanent fixtures. Tonight, Carol was there sitting and talking with them. She looked up as Buck crossed the yard. "Did you hear from Floyd?"

"Floyd? Oh, yeah, Deputy Duckworth. Yes, I did. He's on his

way, escorting Silsbee back here. Raul is over picking them up at the airport."

"Did the sting work?"

Buck got a root beer and sat down in his rocker. "Yes and no. They got a clear admission of guilt on the oilfield thefts even though we didn't need it. They also got him on tape planning to hire somebody to kill me. That's conspiracy to commit murder."

"How about Abernathy?"

"That's the no part. It's clear on the tape that it wasn't him on Abernathy though. We're back to square one on that one."

Carol looked disappointed. "It seemed like such a sure thing. Do you suppose he was telling his brother the truth?"

"It did seem very cut and dried, but I guess things are not always what they seem."

"Let me guess, the minister wants to believe him, but . . ."

"Exactly. The law enforcement officer needs proof."

"So where do you go from here?" Barney asked.

"We still have to look a little deeper into our cheating husband. And we have to start entertaining the idea that it's somebody we don't even have on our radar right now. Maybe we need to spend some more time reading through those files."

"Oh, wonderful," Carol said. "You know how much I love reading through those files."

"Police work is not all glamor and excitement. Much of the time, it's nitpicking investigative work."

"And this is one of those times?"

"I'm thinking it is."

◊

He had it to do. A phone call just wouldn't work. Buck drove out to tell Helen he had her oldest son in his jail, and Jack wasn't going to be getting out for a long time. Sheriff or preacher, the thing he hated the most about either job was having to deliver bad news.

She met him at the door wiping her hands on her apron. "Buck, what a nice surprise. This is getting to be a daily occurrence."

Daily? Had he been coming by daily? That hadn't occurred to him. Did he have this much business out here? Or did he just like coming to see her? "Always the highlight of my day, Helen. But I'd like it better if I wasn't bringing you bad news so much."

"More bad news? Oh, dear."

"Nothing new, I warned you it was going to happen, but I just wanted to let you know I do have Jack in my jail now."

"How bad is it?"

"Harold's plan worked. He did get Jack to confess to the oilfield thefts and conspiring to kill me and got it on tape. He'll do some time, but his brother saved him from the big one. I don't know whether he realizes that yet or not. Maybe he never will get it. Some people are like that."

"Well, I just hate it all the same. I wish there was something I could do."

"The apron strings are cut, Helen, a long time ago. He's charting his own course now."

She put her hand on her forehead. "I suppose so, but it doesn't set well with me."

"Of course not. You wouldn't be you if it didn't bother you."

"Where are my manners? This isn't your fault. Come on in. I have some apple pie cooling. I'll cut you a big slice."

Pretty, and can cook, too. "Sounds good to me. A man would have to be crazy to turn down homemade apple pie."

They settled around the table, and she cut two generous slices. "Whipped cream? I whipped it up fresh while the pie was cooking."

"You're talking my language."

"Coffee?"

"You know, with apple pie, milk would go down right well if you have it."

"I do, freshly milked with the cream skimmed off."

She poured a glass and sat down with him.

"I think this is the best pie I ever put in my mouth."

"I doubt that, but thank you."

"I'm dead serious. You keep feeding me like this, and I may be filling up your doorway every time you turn around."

Suddenly bashful, she looked away but said softly, "Would that be so bad?"

There it was. She was interested. Was he interested? Half the time he had come out, he could have just phoned. He was a confirmed bachelor. But she had called his hand. What should he say? "No, Helen, it wouldn't be bad. It wouldn't be bad at all."

She gave him a shy smile.

I can't leave it hanging. We need to talk about this. "I'm not sure what we're doing here. I just know I like spending time with you, and I seem to be taking just any excuse to get out here. It hasn't occurred to me until this minute, and I mean right this very minute, that there might be something between us. I don't know what it is, but I guess I'm just now trying to wrap my mind around it."

"It came to me earlier, Buck. I'm not sure what is between us either, but I like you, and I'm comfortable with you, and I trust you more than any man I've ever known, even Jiggs."

"I guess there's no hurry to figure it out. We've put it on the table. We can just see where things go."

"When Jiggs passed, I didn't think there would ever be anyone else for me. But you've always been in the picture, always been a friend. Is there more for us? I suppose I can just say I'm open to the idea, and we can go from there."

"How about if the next step we actually go out? Wouldn't that be a good start?"

"Courting? How delightful. I never thought I would be courted again."

"And I've never really courted anyone, so you'll have to excuse me if I don't do it right."

◊

"*What*? Are you kidding me?" Doc leaned forward so far on the bench that Buck was afraid he would fall on his nose. "The Widow Silsbee?"

"No big deal, Doc. We're just exploring the idea that we might have some feelings for each other. Is that so hard to believe?"

"What's hard to believe is the fact that you are just now

figuring it out. We've been watching you spending more and more time out there. Everybody in town figures you two are an item, and now you are telling me you are just discovering it?"

"I couldn't have gotten the word out better if I'd put it on the front page of the paper," Barney added.

Buck shook his head. "I guess I was transparent...to everybody but myself."

Carol went straight to the heart of it. "So, do you love her?"

Buck looked up toward the ceiling of the porch. "Love? No, the 'L' word hasn't been mentioned. Good grief, we just admitted today something else might be there."

"That wasn't the question. I didn't ask if you'd said it; I asked if you've felt it for her."

"Carol, I'm a confirmed bachelor. I'm not sure I even know what love is. I know brotherly love that all believers feel for one another. I get that and surely have that for her. I maybe even have a family sort of love because I was so close to her family for so many years. Yeah, I could admit to that. But a forever, personal 'love-you-till-I-die' kind of love? Who knows, time will tell."

CHAPTER 16

The thousand-yard stare; Buck had it, sitting in the courthouse staring across the lawn toward Main Street, but he didn't really see it. He had a case he needed to be concentrating on, but instead he was sitting here mooning over a female like a teenager with his first love.

Buck sure wasn't a teenager.

But maybe it was his first love.

"Sheriff?"

He swung his chair back around. "Yes."

"It's getting pretty hostile upstairs."

"Hostile?"

"Jack screaming at Roger since he found out he's going to testify against him. Roger is defending himself, again, loudly. The jailers are ready to tie and gag them."

"I better go up and see if I can do anything."

He walked over and opened the door to the private staircase. He could hear them as soon as he opened the door. He walked up and yelled for quiet.

They ignored him.

Buck turned to the jailer and said, "Bring me that fire hose."

The sight of the jailer dragging the end of the fire hose over to Buck caught their attention. Jack said, "What are you doing?"

"You boys seem to be getting overheated. I'm going to cool you down a little."

"Oh, no, you're not."

"And just what do you think you're going to be able to do about it?"

"I'll...I'll...I'll sit down and shut up."

Buck handed the nozzle back to the jailer. "I understand you're yelling at him because he's going to testify against you."

"I'll kill him if he does."

"No, you won't, and you need to quit saying that. You don't get it, do you? We don't even need him. We have your confession on tape. We have dates of bank deposits that coincide with the disappearance of the missing supplies. We have a slam-dunk case, but if he testifies he gets to plea bargain his part of it away. You'd do that in a heartbeat, and you know it."

Jack mumbled something gruffly.

"You're going up for the thefts. You're going up for conspiracy to commit murder. But you ought to go up for being stupid and for disappointing your mother so badly."

"Oh, yeah, I forgot." Jack sneered. "You're a preacher."

"I ought to come up here and regularly practice my sermons. You could use it, and I could use the practice."

"Actually, I'd like that," Roger said.

"Glad to hear that."

◊

Buck came through the staircase door and stopped. His secretary, Sue, came up to him with his cup, now obviously full of coffee. "Good morning, Sheriff."

"Sue, how many times have I told you . . ."

"Give it up, Sheriff, I like to do it for you."

He sighed and took a sip of the coffee, just like he liked it. He looked into her smiling face. She was what one might call pleasantly plump. Not a big woman, but with generous curves, late thirties if he remembered correctly, and always had a smile on her face.

He looked around the office. "If Silsbee is upstairs, then I guess Duckworth just turned him over to Raul at the airport and turned around and went back?"

"Oh, no," she said brightly, "that Houston deputy is here."

"You have him hidden? Shouldn't he be checking in with me?"

"I don't have him hidden, but I suppose Carol does. She met him for breakfast and is showing him the town."

"That oughta take all of five minutes."

"Oh, Sheriff, you're exaggerating." She gave him a playful pat on the arm. "But since this is a county-wide jurisdiction —"

"Yes, I suppose she has to show him the whole county."

Sue looked mischievous. "Do you suppose there might be a little attraction there?"

"Ya think? There was positively electricity in the air when they were together in Houston."

"Did I hear you offered him a job?"

"I did. A chance to get an officer that another department with a big budget has sent through academy and with some big-department experience, however brief it may be, that's a pretty good deal, wouldn't you think?"

"But what if they get serious? Could they both work here?"

"I've thought about that, and I suppose so. There would have to be some rules involved and some scheduling considerations, but, yes, I think it would be okay. We're kinda putting the cart before the horse, though, aren't we?"

"Yes, we are."

He turned and headed for his office. "A lot of that going around," he mumbled.

She heard him. "Are you still talking about Carol and Floyd?"

He paused in his doorway. "I beg your pardon?"

"Oh, Sheriff, everybody knows about you and Helen."

"Apparently, before we did; we just figured out there might be something there yesterday. And still don't know what we have."

"Well, I think it is wonderful, and she is just a delightful lady."

"But she feels more like my sister than somebody I should be courting, and then there is that nagging feeling that I'm stealing Jiggs' wife."

"Jiggs is no longer around to steal from, and he loved both of you so much, I think he would be very happy about it."

"Well, I have a unique idea; how about if we just let these various courtships develop and not start trying to arrange people's lives for them?"

It was the closest she had ever seen Buck come to being testy. He was so even-tempered.

She looked deflated. "I'm sorry, Buck, I'm meddling."

"No, you are concerned, and you care. There's a difference."

The sound of laughing came from the doorway, and Carol and Floyd came sweeping in. Carol was in uniform, but her hair was down, and she had makeup on. She was a cross between the beautiful young lady that went with Buck to Houston and the prim and proper deputy that was always so squared away.

Floyd had done the transfer in uniform but was now dressed in boots and jeans and looked very much at home. He extended his hand as he saw Buck. "Hello, Sheriff."

"I'm guessing there were no problems with the transfer?"

"None at all."

"I see Carol is showing you around?"

"She is. I suppose protocol would be for me to check in with you first, but we had breakfast and—"

Buck silenced him with an upraised palm. "No need to apologize, son, everything is fine. What do you think of your tour?"

"Surprising. Everything in town is nice and green, but you get out in the country, and it is so dry and arid."

"There's a shallow strata of water under the town that people use to water their lawns. It's alkaline and not good to drink, but if you have a hardy type of grass, it works fine for that."

"How interesting."

"I know, more than you wanted to know."

"Actually, Carol mentioned it during her tour."

"I see. Did your Sheriff tell you his thoughts about you thinking along the lines of taking a job here?"

"He did. Apparently, I have the option of taking you up on your offer or staying where I am."

"These days, not everybody gets the chance to choose between jobs. What are you thinking?"

He smiled at Carol. "This area does have a certain appeal."

"I'm sure the appeal is not that arid country out there, but I do think I know what it might be."

A flush of red appeared above his collar. "Am I that obvious?"

"Son, you were that obvious back in Houston. Reckon you two took to each other right off."

"Then I'd like that job if you will have me and if there is no problem with both of us being in the same department."

"The job is yours, and we can work around the problem."

"It'll take me a couple of weeks to wrap things up and get moved."

"I'd expect you to give at least two weeks' notice, so that's fine with me."

Carol said, "Sheriff, we were talking. Since our remaining suspect is in Houston, and he's headed back—"

"Way ahead of you. Son, since you are wrapping things up there, do you suppose you could sandwich in a little work for us? And remember, you would have Mrs. Simmons and that office for the work you would be doing on the side."

"I'd be happy to, sir. Can you bring me up to speed on where things stand?"

"You two come in the office, and we'll go over it."

◊

About the only time Buck wore a suit was when he was preaching, and at funerals and weddings. But he had one on tonight, along with his new silver belly Stetson. He stepped out on the front porch in his full splendor to find the whole group assembled.

A chorus of catcalls greeted him along with applause. "Buck you look positively magnificent," Barney said. "And if I'm not mistaken that's a brand-new tie."

"It is. I thought the occasion demanded it."

Doc scoffed. "A momentous occasion like this, you should have bought a whole new suit."

"I think that would be overkill, Doc."

Buck sat down. He had time yet.

"We've been talking," Barney said. "We've got a lot of years together here on this porch. If you and the widow get hitched, you'd for sure start living out at the ranch. What on earth would we do about our porch?"

"For Pete's sake," Buck laughed. "I'm going on the first date in many a year, and you guys already have me married off? That's ridiculous. But let me set your mind at ease, no matter what, we'll find a way to keep the porch group intact."

"I'm not driving out to the ranch every day," Doc growled.

Buck looked at him. "What is it about 'We'll find a way' that you don't get, Doc?"

"Oh, I dunno. How about what that way might be?"

"You know, Sue and I had this same conversation at the office about Helen and I and about Carol and Floyd. I told her to quit trying to get ahead of things and just let what's going to be develop on its own."

"Floyd and Carol?" Barney asked.

"You mean the rumor mill hasn't gotten around to that one yet? Yes, I have a new deputy, Floyd Duckworth, and he's pretty much coming here because of Carol."

Doc shook his head slowly. "I'm gonna be able to quit watching those soap operas on TV since it is getting plumb interesting right here in my backyard."

CHAPTER 17

Buck picked her up at the ranch. She came to the door wearing a flowered blue, one-piece dress that flattered her slender figure. She invited him in, and he handed her a red rose in a bud vase.

"Why thank you, Buck. How sweet."

Buck stuck a finger in his collar and pulled on it. "I'm a fish out of water here, Helen. I feel like a kid going to his first prom."

She rewarded him with a bright smile. "Those are good metaphors. Do you have any more?"

Even though he was nearly as comfortable in this house as his own, he stayed inside the door with his hat in his hand. "I could probably come up with some more."

"Don't bother; I feel the same way. It never occurred to me that I would find myself dating again. Why are you standing there like a door-to-door salesman, Buck? You'd think you had never been here before."

He moved over to sit down on the couch and watched as she put the bud vase on the mantle. "You know the whole town practically has us married off and probably with a passel of grandkids."

"Really?" Her face showed surprise as she turned around. "You know I don't go into town much; I had no idea. Why would they think that way?" She came over to sit down in the chair facing him.

"Because the rumor mill in a small town is a fearsome thing to behold. And they haven't even turned their attention to Floyd and Carol yet."

"Carol?"

"Yes. To my new deputy that she and I both met while we were in Houston."

"You have a new deputy? He's moving here? Is it because of her?"

"I'm pretty sure it is."

She laughed. "That sounds more substantial than us having a first date, all right."

He stood up. "But surely we aren't going to spend our first date sitting here talking."

She stood up as well and smoothed out her skirt. "I hope not; I'm hungry." She went over to pick up her purse.

"Hungry for anything in particular?"

"I'd kill for some good Mexican food."

"I better head that urge off then. I've already got one murder on my hands that's driving me nuts."

"How is that investigation going?"

"Oh, no. No talking shop tonight. Manuel's Restaurant has been written up in Texas Highways Magazine. I guess it's the top of the line for Mexican food."

"Yes, I love it. Jiggs and I used to go there all the time."

They rode in silence for quite a while before Buck said, "If it was a special place for you and Jiggs, perhaps we should go somewhere else."

"Buck, we are a threesome—you, me and Jiggs. We always

were, and we probably always will be. You were good with that when he was alive, but if you can't do it now, maybe this is not a good idea."

More silence.

Finally, Buck said, "I guess I understand that. I've thought on it some. There are times when you feel more like a sister than someone I might date and also times when I feel like I'm making moves on Jiggs' wife."

"I have the same feelings."

"But then I think he would want you to be happy. In fact, I think he would even want *me* to be happy. He may always be with us, but I'm starting to see him as a benevolent presence. I feel him with his arms around both of us, inviting us to be happy and to move on with our lives."

"What a wonderful mental image." He was focusing on the road, but he could tell she had tears in her eyes. "Yes, I could see him doing that, and I know him—he *would* want us to be happy."

"Then on that happy note, let's set it aside for the evening and have a really good time."

Her face lit up. "I think I can do better than put it aside for the evening."

"How so?"

"I think you have just managed to put me at peace with the whole situation, and I wasn't sure I could ever do that."

He pulled into the parking lot, shut the car off and turned to give her a long look. "I think you're right. I think I even managed to do it to myself.

◊

Duckworth walked into the Harris County Sheriff's office grinning ear to ear. He made his way to the Sheriff's office. As he knocked, the Sheriff looked up, leaned back in his chair, and said, "Don't tell me. I'm losing a deputy."

"I am here to submit my two weeks' notice. Sorry to do it after you spent money on my training and all."

Everly chewed on the stub of a cigar in the corner of his mouth. "You could at least have the courtesy to not look so happy about it."

"I'm sorry, I should—"

The Sheriff held up his hand to stop him. "I'm just ribbing you, Deputy. I didn't ride in here on a turnip truck. I know why you're moving. Love trumps the badge no matter what."

"I didn't say I was in love."

"You didn't say you weren't either. But either way, you won't know until you get out there and pursue it, right?

"That's correct."

He got up and extended his hand. "Congratulations on what *may* be in your future then."

"Thank you."

"Get with Sonny as you wrap things up so he will be up to speed if there is any residual action that will be required."

"Nothing residual about giving traffic tickets out on the interstate."

The Sheriff threw his head back and laughed. "I guess you're right about that. But let me guess, you still have a little work to do for your new department before you leave town?"

"How did you know?"

"Lucky guess."

"I won't let it interfere with my work, sir."

"It is your work; we're still cooperating with Buck on this. But bring Sonny in on it in case more cooperation is required."

"Yes, sir."

◊

Floyd, with Sonny in tow, walked into the Abernathy Detective Agency. Mrs. Simmons looked up and said, "May I help you? Then she recognized Floyd and said, "Oh, you're that deputy that came here with Buck and Carol."

"Yes, ma'am, I am. Buck or I should say Sheriff Green, wants me to update you on the case. I'm actually going to move to Clear Creek and go to work within his department, so I also wanted to introduce Sonny to you, in case more cooperation is needed on the case on this end."

"Pleased to meet you, ma'am."

"I'm sure he told you that Mrs. Abernathy has instructed me to do anything I can to help."

"Is she going to be selling the agency?" Floyd asked.

"Right now, she's thinking of keeping it and maybe hiring some younger investigators to do the field work."

Sonny perked up. "No kidding? I may know some people that would be interested in that. Hey, I may be interested in that myself."

"Oh, no," Floyd said. "If I end up costing the department more deputies, the Sheriff will kill me."

Mrs. Simmons smiled. "Which sheriff are you talking about?"

"Probably both of them."

Sonny looked deep in thought.

Floyd looked back to her and said, "I have some work to do for Buck, seeing if I can find out anything further on this Sessions character."

"That's the guy that was cheating on his wife? Let me get the file."

They went into the conference room and went through the file. The wife, Alice, had hired Abernathy to find the proof that Sessions was cheating.

"When the three of us went to his office, everybody there seemed to know he was cheating on her. It seemed to be quite a matter of interest; I'm betting there is an office pool going."

Mrs. Simmons thumbed through the file. "I'm pretty familiar with all this paperwork, and there's no mention that Delbert ever found out who the third party might be, but he was pretty sure it was someone in Clear Creek."

"As often as Sessions was going to that office, that's a pretty safe bet. I don't think there is anything to be gained by interviewing the wife again, though. I wonder what Buck hoped we might turn up on this end?"

"Over the years, I've learned a lot about how Delbert did his business. I think that's why Mrs. Abernathy wants me to manage the office with some field agents to do the legwork. I say that to say this, if I were sending a field agent to do the next step on this, I would find out the dates that Sessions was in Clear Creek at the time of the murder and preceding it. Then I'd try to find out what women might have been there in hotels on those days and try to rule them out one at a time. I'd also have the agents interview staff to see if somebody might recognize Sessions and remember someone who was there with him."

"That's good thinking."

"As a matter of fact, if we get this agency up and running again, that may be the first thing I assign a field agent to do. Mrs. Abernathy really wants the death of her husband cleared up."

"So you think Sessions is our guy?"

She held the file folder up as an exhibit. "I think he could be. I also think there may be something in these files we are still not seeing, but I do think the answer is here, right in front of us. All we've got right now is Sessions."

Floyd was right with her. "So the next step is for us to go back to Oilfield Supply and have them go into his expense records to find the dates he was in town so we can check with the hotels. There are just a couple of majors there along with some older small units that have been there a long time."

"You know what I think?" she said. "With his generous expense account, I would be highly suspicious if he chose to stay in one of those out-of-the-way places instead of the chain hotels out on the interstate."

"Good point."

◊

They had gotten a list of dates before they called Buck to report.

"I found out most of the time Sessions stayed at the Holiday Inn out on the interstate, but occasionally it would be at the Dixie Lodge Motel over on the old highway. When they asked him about it at work, he told them the larger motels were full, and he had to take what was available."

"That's good work," Buck said over the phone.

"Truthfully, it was Mrs. Simmons' idea. She knows a lot about doing investigations. As a matter of fact, they are talking about keeping the agency open and hiring a couple of investigators to do the legwork for her. The deputy that's with me is even interested."

Buck's voice coming through the receiver was stern. "You threaten to wring his neck if he says anything about it while you're still working together. What he does after you leave is something else, but I don't want the Sheriff there to think I'm costing him more deputies."

Floyd laughed. "We're on a speakerphone; you just threatened him yourself."

"Then that's another thing you need to learn. Never have anyone on a speakerphone without warning them. I like to know who I'm talking to. Hello, Mrs. Simmons."

"Hello, Sheriff."

"We are still very grateful for all your help on this."

"Mrs. Abernathy wants her husband's killer found as much as you do, I suppose even more."

"I understand, and you tell her I have the whole department on it. We're leaving no stones unturned."

"I'll tell her."

Buck hung up the phone and waved Raul in. "I need to send

somebody out to every hotel in town and find out everybody who was there on these dates." He handed him the notes he had made. "Make a copy, I need that back. I need to know if Sessions was registered and I need to know if any women had rooms in their name. We also need to interview the staff. Get a picture of Sessions and show it around to see if anybody remembers seeing a woman with him. Get me a picture of him too. I'm going to take the Dixie Lodge Motel myself."

"The Dixie Lodge?"

"I wanna know why somebody with a big expense account would choose to stay there. And that reminds me, I also want to know if the big hotels were full on any of those nights so someone would have to go elsewhere."

The big deputy turned to go out, but Buck stopped him by adding, "And Raul? I need this yesterday."

CHAPTER 18

The Dixie Lodge Motel was a dated stucco facility with twenty units separated by a covered area like a carport between them. Buck noted it made whatever car parked inside pretty hard to see unless you got up close to them. It was built back in the late thirties when people toured by automobile on trips and vacations.

Mrs. Foley maintained it well, but the units were small and very dated. Still, they were clean and afforded the utmost privacy. At her age, Buck couldn't be sure if she really realized how her clientele had changed over the years or if knew and simply accepted it as inevitable. He doubted that she preferred it that way. When he found her on the little patio next to the office, he got his answer.

"Hello, Mrs. Foley."

She looked up. She was a hefty, elderly lady, who was as much a fixture in town as her dated old motel. "Why, hello, Buck. I don't see you very often these days."

"We could remedy that if you'd come to my church on Sunday."

"Why, bless your heart, I would dearly love that, but this place is open 24/7 you know. I haven't had a day off in so long I wouldn't know how to act. Come sit down. You want some coffee?"

Buck took a seat. "I just had some, thank you. I understand

about 24/7, our office has to deal with that, too. However, I also know that being away for an hour on Sunday morning probably wouldn't be a problem. Your guests are either up much earlier, or they sleep in."

She laughed. "You're probably right. Over the years, my guests have changed, and not many seem to spend the whole night anymore."

He studied her face as he asked, "Does that bother you?"

"No, I can't live other people's lives for them, and what they choose to do is their own business." She waved a finger at him. "Now if I had some woman try to set up shop in one of my rooms, I wouldn't sit still for that, but . . ."

Buck laughed, "No, I know you'd toss somebody like that out on their ear."

She seemed to make up her mind. "I *will* try to get to services, Buck. When you start missing them, it can get easier and easier to find excuses."

"It surely can."

"Is that why you're here? Making a visitation for your church?"

"It is, but I also have a little business to conduct."

She looked mildly suspicious. "Bible business or badge business? I can't really afford much of a donation these days."

"No, I'm not here with my hand out. I don't generally solicit businesses for donations for the church anyway. My people are self-sustaining." He pulled a picture from his pocket. "I know that Steve Sessions stays here on occasion."

She took the picture. "Yes, I recognize him; he's been here

several times. And you want to know if there was anybody with him?"

"How very perceptive of you."

"He comes with Susan Brown."

Buck was stunned. "You actually have a name?"

"Of course. I know Susan. I see her at the grocery store all the time. I'm a little disappointed that she's running around with a married man, but that is none of my business."

"You know he's a married man?"

"Don't be naïve, Buck. If he wasn't married, they would be staying out at one of the hotels on the interstate."

"You are a marvel."

"Don't mistake acceptance for approval. I know what goes on in my rooms, and I don't approve, but I have to make a living. I don't approve of a lot of things going on in our country these days. We have people calling evil good and people calling good evil. That isn't right, but I'm not in charge. There's nothing I can do about it, except to vote when it comes time, and I fear that vote isn't changing much."

"You are so right, and you would fit in at our church very well. I hope you will come see us."

"I think I will, Buck. I think I will."

◊

"Raul, you aren't going to believe this."

"Sheriff, these days I believe just about anything."

"I went out to check with Mrs. Foley, and with no prompting at all, she just laid the name of the mystery woman on me."

"Okay, you're right; I don't believe it. That's too good to be true. She's the woman at the crime scene?"

"We don't know that, but she is the third leg of the Steve Sessions love triangle."

"That's a good thing because everybody drew a blank at the other facilities, registrations, and interviews. Except we did find out he could have had a room out on the interstate if he had wanted."

"I expected that as soon as I heard what Mrs. Foley had to say, but we needed to make sure."

"Are we going to go talk to her?"

"Absolutely, but for appearance sake, I need Carol with me instead of two guys going."

"I'll call her in."

It took about twenty minutes for Carol to get back to the office and for them to head over to the Brown home. She came to the door dressed as if she had just come home from work. She was a brunette, middle-aged woman, and looked to be in her late forties or early fifties. Buck looked at his watch and surmised she was home for lunch.

"Mrs. Brown? I'm Sheriff Green, and this is Deputy Tatum. May we come in?"

"Is something wrong? Is it my husband? Has something happened to him?"

So there is a husband, Buck thought. *Not a triangle but a square.* "Nothing to do with your husband, ma'am. We're here to talk to you about Steve Sessions."

She was leading them into the living room when he said it, but

136

spun around, wide-eyed. "Steve? Oh no, what—"

"Nothing has happened to him either, but we know you are having a relationship with him. We know about the meetings over at the motel."

"Oh, we can't talk about that here." She was suddenly very flustered. "My husband. You don't understand; he's so jealous and has a terrible temper. If he found out… Oh, my."

"We have to talk about it here, or at the office," Buck said brusquely. "We can take you in for questioning."

She flushed red. "That won't be necessary. I'll meet you there in ten minutes or so. I never know when Ken may be home. He drops in now and then, particularly at lunch time."

"It sounds to me like he suspects something."

"Maybe. I don't know." She was clearly extremely flustered. "Oh, I don't know how I ever got involved in this, but I can't seem to get out of it. I love Steve, Sheriff. I know it's wrong, but I do." She rushed over to the closet. "But we have to go. We have to go right now. We can't talk about it here."

Back in the car, the door had hardly closed before Carol said, "A very violent husband who suspects something?"

"I'd say we have a brand-new suspect."

◊

Susan Brown clutched her handbag so tightly that her knuckles were white. "This is so embarrassing."

Carol was still with them, sitting in the chair beside the woman, while Buck was in his chair behind the desk; proper protocol for a female suspect. Buck answered, "I can see how it would be that way."

"It started so innocently. I work in the office at Oilfield Supply, and Steve would come around, and he was something of a flirt."

Buck mentally kicked himself. *Are you kidding me? Oilfield Supply? Why didn't I think to start with the women right in his branch office? I have to be the dumbest Sheriff in history.*

"Go on."

"Then a couple of times, we went out to eat. We had too much to drink one time, and we ended up in his hotel room. That was the start of it, and it got easier after that. He started calling on this office more and more."

"Funny how that works," Buck said unsympathetically. "Tell me about your husband."

"Ken is a ticking time bomb. He can be sweet, but the next minute, he can be completely out of control. It can happen in a heartbeat, and he can be so...so very violent."

"Does he hurt you?" Carol asked softly.

"When he's in such a state, yes. Yes, he can. I try not to get him angry."

"I'm sorry," Buck said, his tone changing. "But I can't say cheating on him is trying very hard."

Tears came into her eyes. "No, that's true. You don't understand, Sheriff, after years of living with all the violence, the chance to be with someone who showed me some compassion and some tenderness was too much to pass up. It was addictive. I couldn't give it up."

"Why haven't you left him?" Carol asked.

Her eyes widened. "Oh, I couldn't do that. He'd kill me. He's told me so."

"Have you ever heard of a private investigator by the name of Delbert Abernathy?"

"Yes, he was in our office several times investigating some stolen oilfield equipment. He got killed, didn't he?"

"Yes, and there was a woman in the car with whoever did the killing." Watching closely for her reaction he pulled the pin on the grenade and lobbed it into the room. "Mrs. Brown, were you that woman?"

"*What?*" Her eyes got wide, and her voice rose as she came half out of her chair. Carol put a hand on her arm to calm her. She started sobbing. "Is that what you think? Is that why I'm here? I could never—"

The reaction seemed genuine to Buck. He studied her face as she reacted. She continued to sob, distraught, she seemed like she had painted herself into a corner and now could not find her way out.

The phone rang. Buck picked it up. "I said I didn't want to be disturbed."

Raul said, "I think you do. I have Steve Sessions out here. He just walked in the door."

"Bring him in."

When Sessions came in the door, Mrs. Brown jumped into his arms, and they stood locked in an embrace, her sobbing into his chest. Raul pushed another chair through the door then left, closing it behind him.

Finally, they separated and took seats.

Buck looked at Sessions and came right to the point, "Why are you here?"

"I called on our office here, and Susan wasn't there. They said she hadn't come back from lunch. I swung by her house and didn't see her car, but a couple of neighbors were standing out talking. They told me a police car had been at the house, and when it left she left, too. The neighbors know about her husband's temper and were afraid something had happened. I went by the police station, but they didn't know anything about it so I came here."

Susan said softly, "Steve, they know."

"Know what?"

"Know about our affair."

He sighed deeply. "It had to come out some time I guess."

Buck studied him closely as he asked, "Did you confront the private investigator over it?"

"He was investigating oilfield thefts, not me."

Buck shook his head. "I'm afraid you're wrong there. He was doing both."

"He was?"

"Your wife hired him."

"Alice knows?"

Buck thought his action appeared to be genuine. "She suspects. He was to give her the proof she needs to divorce you."

"The way we've been living together the past few years all she would have to do is ask."

Time to go in for the big one. "Mr. Sessions, did you kill Delbert Abernathy?"

"Of course not. Why would I do that?"

"Maybe because he was getting too close to your affair?"

"I didn't even know he was investigating me. And even now, I only have your word that he was. Besides, getting caught cheating is hardly grounds for somebody to get killed."

Susan sobbed. "They think you did it, and they think I helped."

Sessions had gone from being defensive to being upset. "Ridiculous. You are completely off base here."

"Maybe. We'll see."

Anger showed in his face. "Whatever you think, you have blown this situation sky high. If I could find out so quickly where Susan was, you can bet by now her husband knows as well."

"But he doesn't know of the affair. We can just tell him we had her down here in connection with the oilfield thefts."

Sessions shook his head. "I don't think you can count on him buying that. You don't understand how dangerous the man is. I think you've put her life in danger now."

This is taking a turn of events I didn't expect. That's why these domestic situations are so unpredictable. "What do you suggest?"

Sessions had a ready answer. "How about if I take her over to Midland and check her into a room under my name. Hide her away until we can figure something out."

Buck nodded but was a little skeptical. "If you two think that is best. But stay in touch with this office. If you try to go on the run, we'll be coming after you."

"No problem, Sheriff. It's time we faced this. I'm sorry if I sounded accusatory. Actually, you may have just forced us to go ahead and deal with it. If only I knew how."

"We'll figure out how," Buck said. "One more thing, Mrs. Brown. Is your husband capable of killing that private investigator?"

"I don't believe he had anything to do with it but is he capable of it? Yes."

"For that to happen, he had to know what Abernathy was investigating, which means he had to know about the affair. Has he been different toward you lately?"

"He's been very sullen, but he has his moods, so it's hard to say." She shuddered. "If he knew, I don't think I would still be alive."

Buck continued to press. "How about if he knew, but couldn't find out who the man was? Could he be biding his time trying to get a name?"

"He could be capable of that."

"How about if he confronted the private investigator, but the man refused to tell him? Could that set him off?"

"Without a doubt." She sat and thought about it. "My God, he did it."

CHAPTER 19

Buck stood in the window of his office and watched them drive off. He wondered if he was doing the right thing. His secretary buzzed him, and he answered.

"The Police Chief on line two for you."

He picked up the handset. "Hello, Sam, what can I do for you?"

"I've got a husband over here filing a missing person's report."

"Okay, how long has the person been missing?"

"Didn't return to work after lunch. I know a routine missing person report isn't filed for 72 hours unless it's a child or there is some other compelling reason."

"So why are you calling me?" Buck asked.

"Because this is the second time in a couple of hours someone has come in hunting this lady. I sent the first one over to you."

"You're talking about Susan Brown."

"I am."

"Between us, the woman is in danger and in witness protection as a material witness. Her husband cannot know where she is right now."

"I understand."

"Is he sitting right there?"

"Outside my office. I told him I have nothing but would check with you."

"I don't want to lie to the man, can you tell him you checked with me, and we had nothing to report at this time?"

"I can do that, that exact wording. And Buck? You owe me one."

Buck hung up the phone. His gut told him Brown was implicated in this, but how? His violent temper didn't seem to mesh with him patiently waiting to confront his wife. And if it was him, who was the woman? Still too many unanswered questions.

The buzzer sounded again. "Yes?"

"Helen is on line one for you, Sheriff."

That was a distraction he needed right now. "Hello."

"Buck, Jimmy is here, and he has his business plan for the ranch finished. When could you take a look at it?"

"How about right now? I could use a break. I'll be right out."

◊

They were sitting in the living room when he arrived. They each had a bound presentation folder in their hands, and there was a third one on the table waiting for him. He opened the cover. "This looks very professional."

"I've been consulting with my professors for days. I wanted to do the best job that I could. You will see that I have addressed each of your 'variables,' with research and figures to back them up. The cover letter is what I would put on it for presentation to a bank for a loan."

He gave them a moment to read the letter.

Buck smiled. "This will be very helpful if we find a need to secure some additional funding for something. Go on."

Jimmy turned the page. "Variable number one, you mentioned access to an expert investment advisor with a vested interest in the ranch, in short, Harold."

"Yes, I believe it is important for him to have an active role."

"I believe implementation of this plan will produce some significant income, much of which will be plowed back in, but also some reserves that will need some expert handling. That is spelled out here."

"Exactly what I had in mind."

Jimmy told them to turn the page. "Variable number two was the possibility of oil development. Jack had in mind doing wildcatting on his own, which could produce far greater revenues but which would have far greater risk. He had, after all, made and run through several fortunes in his time in the oilfields."

"Plus the fact that he won't be available for a good while."

"There is that," Jimmy agreed, "and in retrospect, I see you knew it was coming when you indicated his role could change. We didn't catch what you were saying at the time of course. What I propose instead is a leasing arrangement that puts the risk of exploration, along with a lion's share of the profits, in the hands of a major drilling concern. I have had a dialogue with a number of them and have selected the top three contenders and put them in here. That should produce a very lucrative, but very stable return, and I am assured that our ranch is located in the middle of a proven area, so the chances of success are very great indeed."

"Again, precisely what I hoped you would come up with."

"Next page, variable number three, ranch operations. This is my main area of study over the past few years, and I'm eager to get on with it. The brothers wanted to basically divest the ranch operations since they were break-even at best. They were correct; it is break-even now. But what they failed to grasp is it doesn't have to be."

"Your father realized that. That's why he sent you off to school to learn what the ranch needed."

"And I did. The livestock inventory has been dwindling for some time. We need to invest in some good breeding stock. Instead of buying hay to feed over the winter, we need to put some of the land into cultivation to produce our own winter feed. My calculations show we could easily do that, and with the number of cuttings that we can get in this area, could have a tidy income from selling surplus, as well. We have sufficient water rights to do the livestock and the farming. We would need to do some upgrading of equipment, which might necessitate some short-term capital, but Harold could help us with that."

"I think your father's investment in you has paid off."

"Finally, to set everyone's mind at ease on my age, experience, and management skills, I plan to incorporate the ranch with the family as the board of directors. Any major financial transactions, purchases or decisions would require the approval of the Board. Given your position in the situation, Buck, barring any changes, I propose you be on that board as well and serve as the chair."

"Very sensible and with my role, for now, would be appropriate."

Jimmy closed his folder. "That's the main points. There are a lot of other specifics, time frames, requirements, all spelled out in detail. This operation should be producing income within the year and build from there. Barring serious weather or economic conditions, this ranch should never be break-even again, and Harold's shrewd handling of our reserves should prepare us for even that."

"Helen, what do you think?"

"I think it's wonderful. I am so proud."

"As you should be. So you approve of going ahead with this plan?"

"Wholeheartedly."

Buck clasped his hands together. "All right, here's the next step. I want you to go meet with Harold and Linda and walk them through this just as you did us. Tell them we are both on board. My feeling is they will have a whole new respect for you when you finish."

"How about Jack?" Jimmy looked concerned. Buck was sure it meant he did not relish going to make the presentation to his older brother.

"I'll talk to Jack. When you get the approval of the other two, we can start moving forward with your plan."

Jimmy hesitated. "I haven't said anything, but I guess I can now. The missing money and livestock? We're pretty sure that was Jack."

"We're pretty sure of it, too, but like you, I chose not to pursue it. I figured your audit would turn it up. Now one last thing, how about your ranch foreman?"

"I've already shared the ranch portion of the plan with him, and he gave me some input on it. He's as excited as I am about moving forward with it, and he's a good man."

"I know. Your dad trusted him completely, but I wanted you to form your own opinion."

"He'll do."

◊

Jack was still in jail awaiting trial. Buck had him brought down. With the feelings he harbored toward him, Buck didn't fully trust Jack, so Raul sat in on the meeting. The sullen demeanor was gone. He seemed defeated, depressed.

"I could have come up there to talk to you, but I thought you'd appreciate being out of the cage for a bit."

"Yeah, thanks," he said in a flat voice devoid of emotion.

"I wanted you to see something." He pushed a copy of the business plan across the desk. "I asked your brother to work this up. It's a business plan for the development of the ranch."

Jack picked it up, and Buck started to walk him through it just as Jimmy had done.

When he finished, Jack said, "I didn't know the little twerp had it in him. This could actually work."

"Yes, I believe it will. Your father did, too, it's why he sent him to school to learn what he needed to know to do this."

Jack sat there for a long time, looking through the proposal and thinking. Buck waited him out. Finally, he sighed deeply. "I've really messed up." He tossed the proposal back on the desk. "I could have been a part of this."

Buck tossed the proposal back. "Keep that. You still are a part of it. Your share will be put in escrow for you until you get out, but with a provision on it that you have to straighten up and fly right. A seat on that Board of Directors is yours, but only if you can earn the trust of your family again, particularly after you stole from them."

"You know about that, huh? Why wasn't I charged with it?"

"The whole family knew but didn't want to do it. I had the evidence but respected their wishes. You see, Jack, your brothers did you a great favor. Harold kept you from committing a crime that would have put you in jail for a long time, maybe even life or the death sentence. Jimmy stepped up and saw to it that the family theft wasn't added to your burden. Your mother and sister were in total agreement."

"I don't deserve that."

"No, you don't. But there is a difference between forgiveness and trust. They have forgiven you and do love you, but honestly, they don't trust you. All of us will ensure that you aren't in a position to do it again. And of course, that also means not putting temptation in your path."

"I understand. I messed up. I have to earn my way back."

"You've messed up all right and will have to pay for it, but it doesn't have to ruin your entire life. Take the time while you are incarcerated to do what Jimmy did and take advantage of educational opportunities. Come out prepared to step up and play a role, and the family will welcome you back. You know what changes you have to make to your attitude to be deserving of that. Make them!"

Jack nodded slowly as if the idea was sinking in. "I got a lot to make up for."

"Jack, most people don't get a genuine second chance at life, but I believe you are going to have just that. Make sure you make the most of it."

◊

Jimmy was still there when Buck went back out to the ranch to report on his meeting with Jack. He told them what he had said to Jack and how he responded. "Maybe he will turn his life around," Helen said. "Oh, how I hope so."

"I think there's a good chance of it. I want you to relay that to the other two when you go see them, Jimmy. Tell them what I told him and above all tell them how he reacted."

Jimmy grinned. "That's not all I have to tell them."

"What do you mean?

"I plan to tell them that you and mother have become an item."

Buck put his hand on the back of his neck and looked rather sheepish. "You've been talking to her, huh?"

"I have. We tell each other everything. I'm her favorite."

She laughed. "I've never said that, but we are very close. Just between us, probably closer than any of the rest. He was my baby after all."

"Well just to make things perfectly clear I wouldn't say your mother and I are an item. I'd say maybe we are *talking* about being an item. But if we were, how would you feel about that?"

"You've always been family, Buck. She told me about how you and she and dad are a trio and about him putting his arm around you and telling you it's okay. I can see him doing that, and

I think he would approve if he could tell us. I plan to pass that on to the others as well."

Buck clasped a hand on his shoulder. "You're turning into quite the man, Jimmy. I'm very proud of you, and I know your mama is."

CHAPTER 20

Buck walked into the squad room. "Is Sessions still checking in?"

Raul looked around and spoke in a conspiratorial tone. "He's staying in touch. Nobody knows where they are but you and me."

"Let's keep it that way, but we can't go on like that forever. We've got to find a way to resolve this."

"We aren't tailing Brown, but all units know to do drive-bys when they are close to his home or at work. They report what they see, and Penny is keeping a log. He's not paying much attention to the fact that his wife is missing."

"He's playing it mighty close to the vest."

"You think we're betting on the wrong horse here?" Raul said.

"It could be. The only problem is, we can't let this become a one-horse race. I just have this nagging feeling that we're so focused on this guy, we can't see what else is out there. We still have uncorroborated stories. It seemed to be going one way and then seemed to be going another. We've got to nail this thing down with proof before we can go to court."

"A one-horse race, and you're having a nag feeling?"

"Nagg*ing.* Put the 'ing' on it…"

"Just couldn't resist," Raul said. "But seriously, Buck, I've read in those silly files until I nearly have them memorized. If there's something else there, I just don't see it."

Buck agreed. "I'm the same way, but I keep telling myself we pursued the obvious connections. Maybe we're looking for one that isn't obvious. But if so, I don't know how to find it. Right now, we may only have one horse in the race, but he's looking pretty good for it."

"It's the woman I keep coming back to." Raul rubbed his neck in thought. "Who was the woman? If we knew that, this might all fall into place."

"I've entertained the idea a couple of times that it might be Alice Sessions, but I talk myself out of it."

Raul didn't get that one. "How?"

"Think about it, Alice Sessions didn't know who the woman was that her husband was messing with. That's what she was paying Abernathy to find out. So, if Brown is our guy and Alice was the woman, it would mean she *did* know the woman, and it would also mean he knew who his wife was seeing. That makes no sense. Brown would have gone ballistic, and he isn't doing that."

"That's good logic. Could we construct any kind of scenario where it would make sense?"

Buck smiled. "I've chased that coon around the tree more than once. It might make sense if instead of divorcing her husband, she hired Brown to kill him."

"I could see that. He couldn't get too aggressive toward her husband in public if he wanted to kill him in private. But we have nothing that points to that being planned."

"No, I'm just spit-balling, but for sure, he couldn't get after his wife because that would be a tip-off that he knew."

"I think you might have something there."

"But there's still a problem." Buck rubbed his forehead as if the heavy thinking was starting to get to him. "Why kill the PI? Abernathy doesn't appear to have known either name. He wasn't a threat to anybody."

"What if he did know? The crime scene showed that Abernathy was driven out there in his assailant's car. What if she came out, and he met with her to tell her what he had found. What if he got there to find out he was meeting with both of them?"

Buck shrugged. "If she had already worked out to kill Sessions, that would make Abernathy a big loose end."

"So what do we have to prove, and how do we do it?"

"I have an idea." He reached for the phone and dialed Abernathy's office in Houston. When she answered he said, "Florence, has Mrs. Sessions asked for any progress reports on her case."

"No, she hasn't."

"After he died did she ask you if he left any notes or anything that might name her husband's mistress?"

"Not that either."

"Does it strike you as a little odd that she didn't make one last effort to see if the investigation had born fruit? Particularly when she knew he had been killed in the town where the woman would be?"

"I hear what you are saying, Buck, it's almost as if—"

"Almost as if she already knew the answer. Thank you Florence."

Buck hung up.

Raul frowned. "What does that prove?"

"By itself, nothing. But it takes a lot of pieces to put a puzzle together."

"She's still claiming to this day that she doesn't know who the woman was."

"Exactly. Which means she couldn't know the woman's husband was either." Buck clasped his hand over his mouth as he thought. "We need another piece."

He picked up the phone and called Duckworth. When he answered, Buck said, "You up for a little more investigative work?

"Sure, I'm just home packing. What do you need?"

"You remember Mrs. Sessions?"

"Yes, sir."

"And you'd recognize her if you saw her?"

"I would."

"I'm going to have her meet someone at a restaurant somewhere. Somewhere innocuous. You have any suggestions?"

"There's a Denny's Restaurant that would be close to her. That would be pretty nondescript."

"Perfect. I need you to be there at 3 pm tomorrow. If she shows, I just need you to take her picture waiting. Nothing else, just prove she showed."

"No problem."

Buck hung up the phone. "If she bites that'll prove she does know Brown. Get one of those burner phones from that drug bust and send her a text saying 'will be in town and must talk – the Denny's by your house tomorrow 3 pm and sign it Ken.' I'm going to go see the judge and get permission to wiretap his phone."

"Got it, but can they tap into cell phone calls?"

"The phone company can."

"You think it'll work?"

"Who knows, if it does we'll have another puzzle piece. If it works REALLY well one of them may say something incriminating. If it doesn't work at all, we may have to face the idea that we're barking up the wrong tree again and no matter how it looks he may not be our guy."

◊

It was just Doc and Barney on the porch tonight. "Okay, Buck, you're holding out on us," Barney said.

"On the case?"

"That and how your date went the other night."

"I'd rather know about the date," Doc injected. "That might more directly affect our future."

"Now Doc, I told you I'm going to take steps to protect the porch gathering."

"What kind of steps?"

"Oh I have a couple of options so don't worry about it."

Doc looked down, shaking his head slowly side to side. "Well I do worry about it, confound it. This time, every day is important to me."

Barney agreed. "It's important to all of us, Doc. So how did it go, Buck?"

"Her son said he had heard we were becoming an 'item.' I told him we were talking about *maybe* becoming an item. People sure are wanting to rush things."

"So no progress to report?"

"I wouldn't say that, Barney. We did find a way for both of us to come to terms with our prior relationship and are comfortable with that now. That's huge."

"You're going to have to define 'prior relationship,'" Barney said.

"It was always a threesome with her husband, Jiggs."

"And now it isn't?"

"There may always be a threesome, but we've figured out how to come to terms with it."

"Well that's just plumb silly," Doc sputtered. "Who ever heard of such a thing?"

"I'll walk you through it, Doc. It makes perfect sense."

CHAPTER 21

Raul came in to report. "Everything is set up, Sheriff. We got the warrant. The phone company has the trap on his phone to record any calls. We've got a car watching Brown. The text was sent. It's all in place."

"I just talked to Duckworth. He's in place. Nothing to do now but wait."

Raul set down. "What do we do if this doesn't work out?"

"If we're after the wrong guy we just have to go back to hunting the right guy."

"That thought just makes me tired. We've already had a couple of absolute cinches fall through."

"Maybe as they say the third time is the charm."

They sat there in silence for a while, both lost in thought. Then the phone rang, and Buck picked it up. "Hello."

"Sheriff, this is Deputy Duckworth."

"Don't be so formal, you can be Floyd except when we are on the job and in front of people. And you can call me Buck. So what do you have?"

"She showed, Sheriff...err, Buck. I took her picture waiting. I made it a short video, and I scanned the room to also show the clock and the calendar on the wall."

"Good work. She didn't see you doing all that?"

"No sir, she was very focused on the parking lot. I think she was expecting to meet somebody and maybe go out and catch them before they came in. That's the feeling I had anyway."

"Excellent, go back to your packing. I'll holler if I need you. We're looking forward to having you here, you're a good man."

"Thank you, sir."

Buck hung up the phone and looked at Raul. "One more piece to the puzzle. The next piece may make us or break us. We'll go over to where they have the tap set up and listen there after five."

"Where is it?"

"They're going to forward any calls to our phone. We'll be able to hear both sides of the conversation, and they'll be recording it as well. We'll get over there and watch the back of the house in the alley."

They sat there in the alley for a good while before Raul's radio said, "This is unit six. Suspect's vehicle is pulling into his driveway."

"This is unit two, 10-4, we'll take it from here. Park down the street and keep an eye on the front."

They were beginning to think their grand scheme hadn't worked when suddenly the phone rang. They sat up eagerly. The recorder started automatically, and a man's voice came over the speaker.

"Hello."

They recognized Brown's voice.

"Oh, hello, is Susan there?"

"No she's away for a few days, may I ask who is calling?"

"This is Sandy at the office. She hasn't been at work for several days, and we're getting worried about her."

"She got called away unexpectedly on a family emergency. I

guess she didn't think to call before she left. I'll have her get in touch with you."

"We understand about family emergencies, but she really should have called in."

"Yes, I agree with you. I'll tell her."

"Well, all right. Goodbye."

The line went dead.

"That was a bust," Raul said.

"Not entirely."

"How so, Sheriff?"

"That's a pretty lame excuse about where his wife is. The Ken Brown everyone tells me about should have bit her head off and hung up on her. Instead, he takes the time to make nice and lie about where she is."

"What does that mean?"

"I don't know, but it's another puzzle piece, even if it is a small one."

Thirty minutes later the phone rang again. "Helllllo."

"Sounds like he's been drinking," Buck said.

"Ken, is that you? You don't sound like yourself."

"Of coursh it's me. Who else would answer my phone?"

"Oh dear, you've been drinking. Is that why you didn't meet me?"

Raul nudged Buck in the ribs, and he nodded at him.

"Say, who . .. who is this?"

"This is Alice."

Buck pumped a fist. Puzzle piece.

"Alice?"

"Alice Sessions. Maybe I had better call back when you are sober."

"Aw man," Buck said. "It's like he's working for us. He even got her to say her full name."

Brown's brain seemed to start working. "Alice?" Then it apparently registered. "Oh my god, what are you calling me for, don't you know—"

"You texted me to meet you at Denny's. It sounded important. I thought maybe you had found them and done the job."

"Text you? I've never texted anybody in my life. Don't you know what this means? Get off the phone. Get off right now."

The phone went dead again.

"Not a slam-dunk confession," Buck said. "But a big puzzle piece, and with the right evidence support it, her saying 'I thought maybe you had found them and done the job.' Might do it. It might be enough. Besides, she even set up a confirmation of Duckworth's video."

The back gate to Brown's place opened and he staggered out. He looked up and down the alley, spotted the patrol car and aimed the shotgun.

"HIT THE DECK," Buck yelled.

The front windshield was peppered with a volley of bird shot. Buck and Raul bailed out the doors, leaving them open for cover. "It's just bird shot," Raul yelled.

"Birdshot will mess you up if he gets close enough," Buck shouted, "and he's coming."

They both raised up where he could see them and in unison yelled. "DROP THAT WEAPON OR WE'LL FIRE."

He leveled the shotgun on Buck who ducked behind the fender as he heard the pellets ricochet off the metal. Brown worked the slide again and advanced on Buck.

Raul raised up and fired.

Brown went down.

They both ran to secure the weapon.

Raul rolled him over and cuffed him roughly. "Owwww, my shoulder."

"You're lucky it wasn't between your eyes. If you fire on an officer, you better know we're going to fire back."

"Let's take him by the clinic. I'll call Doc to meet us."

He made the call, then he made another call. "Duckworth? Arrest Sessions and get on a plane with her. The charge? Conspiracy to commit murder."

◊

Brown was lying on a metal table while Doc pulled a bullet out with a pair of forceps. "The body is a wonderful machine," he said, "then along comes the invention of the gun and messes everything all up."

Buck grinned. "I think I just heard Doc on Gunsmoke say those exact same words on a rerun episode."

"I shouldn't wonder, I watch those old episodes all the time. Have them all recorded."

"No wonder you sound more and more like him all the time. I think you wish you really were living back in the old West."

"I do, for a fact, Buck. Those were simpler times. Black was black and white was white and there were clear lines between good and evil. There weren't nearly as many laws on the books, but everybody knew what justice was, and if it didn't exist, they made it right themselves."

"That's a pretty idealized view of what was a pretty complex time in our history."

"It's the view I care to have, and I intend to stick with it." He finished putting a good size bandage on the wound. "There, didn't hit anything major. He'll heal, but his right arm is going to be mighty sore for quite a while."

"Take him back to the jail and book him, Raul." He pulled the big man over to the side. "We've got his accomplice on the way from Houston. I don't want the two of them in the same jail where there is any chance they can talk together. Our cells are not that private. I'm going to stop and talk to the Chief and arrange for them to house Mrs. Sessions at the city jail until we can get her into the women's facility out at the prison. The city jail ought to do the job in the meantime."

CHAPTER 22

"What's your plan Sheriff?" Raul was framed in his doorway. "We go to work interrogating Brown?

"We'll see what we can get from him later, but Mrs. Sessions is the key. This will make three strikes for Brown. If he goes in, he's not coming back out, and he knows it. We can't offer him any kind of deal, and he knows that too. Besides, it would make no sense to offer a deal to a killer to implicate someone who was an accomplice."

"So you plan to talk to Sessions first?"

"I do. I've sent Carol over to the city jail for her. If I can get her to see what she is facing, maybe I can offer a reduced sentence to testify against Brown. And she may give us something we can use to break Brown."

"We're about to find out, here comes Carol."

Buck was surprised to turn and see the woman coming in wearing handcuffs. Instead of the well-manicured, well-dressed woman he had met in Houston, this woman looked beaten. She had on no makeup and her hair was in disarray. Instead of feeling sympathy Buck found himself thinking: *This is good. This is a woman who may listen. She may be willing to take some kind of deal.*

Carol took her into the interrogation room. Buck went in and sat down. She had a hollow, vacant look. "Mrs. Sessions, would you like a drink of water?"

"Water? Yes, water would be good."

They brought her a bottle of water, and she drank it hungrily, over half of it without taking it from her lips.

"Mrs. Sessions, for the record you have been read your rights?"

"Yes."

"You know you can be represented by an attorney?"

"Yes."

"Have you contacted your attorney?"

"I don't have one."

"If you can't afford one, one will be provided for you."

"I can afford one. But I don't need one, I haven't done anything."

Buck tried to get her to focus. "Your life has turned upside down pretty quickly."

She nodded slowly but did not answer.

"I bet it never occurred to you that you would be locked up in jail."

Her voice was barely above a whisper, "I don't know why this is happening to me, I've done nothing."

"That's the way you are going to play it, huh? Mrs. Sessions, we have all we need to convict you. We even have your phone call to Brown asking him if the job had been done."

"That doesn't mean...I mean...he was doing some work for me."

"Yes he was, and we know what kind of work it was. The jury will not have to have it spelled out for them."

"This can't be happening."

"But it is happening, Mrs. Sessions, and you have no one to blame but yourself. You're going to jail, there is no doubt about it."

"I can't—"

"You have no choice in the matter."

She began sobbing softly, her shoulders heaving.

"You may be able to reduce your sentence, though. You may be able to even get incarcerated in a facility that offers better amenities."

Her tear-filled eyes made contact with his, then suddenly hardened. "This is not right. I'm the victim here." She rose half-way out of her chair and raised her voice. "He cheated on ME! I'm the victim here!"

"Yes. Yes, he did. But your response was totally inappropriate. It was highly against the law and what he did to you pales in comparison. Can't you see that?"

She lowered herself back into her chair, and the fire went out of her eyes. "I don't know what happened to me. I don't know why—"

"Why what?"

"Why I ever thought getting Ken to do away with my husband was a good idea. It seemed to make sense at the time."

BINGO! If what we had on her was not strong enough this recording should nail the lid on them both.

"I get the feeling you are getting resigned to what is going to happen. Are you ready to talk about a deal?"

She sat there for a bit, then finally said "I think I've made a mistake. I think I need to talk to an attorney."

"That's your right and has been all along. We'll stop now and arrange for someone to represent you. Carol, can you attend to that? We'll take it back up when she has a lawyer beside her."

Carol led her out. Raul said, "She should have done that in the beginning."

"Yes, she should have, but the lawyer is just going to advise her to take the deal, you know that."

"If they are worth their salt they will."

◊

Buck sat staring out the window. Raul knew the look. He was deep in thought.

"Is that rubber I smell burning?"

Buck knew what he meant. "No, it's just me grinding the gears of my brain."

"Whatcha thinking about so hard?"

"There's something nagging at me. Mrs. Sessions had an alibi. We dismissed her as a suspect because the hospital put her in Houston at the time of the murder. We now know she wasn't. A good lawyer could pull that card out of the deck at the trial."

"What do you want to do?"

"Duckworth is loading his things on a truck to move today, right?"

"Yes, he'll probably be driving back tomorrow."

"Get him on the phone, he has one last job to do. I'm going to call the judge."

Buck made his call then got on the line with Duckworth.

"How's the moving going?"

"Fine."

"I understand you have help?"

"You know Carol came with me to help."

"Yes, I'm sure that is making the work lighter if you can concentrate on what you are doing. You have a place to move to?"

"A small apartment. Just temporary until I get my bearings. And until I see if there are going to be any major changes in my life."

"I understand what you are saying. Very prudent. Listen, I need one or both of you to go back out to that hospital. Last time we tried to check Mrs. Sessions' alibi, it was just a casual request. I just had the judge fax a subpoena for material evidence to them, and I think they will be more forthcoming now. We need to know the exact times and places now."

"Will do."

"You kids don't work too hard."

"We won't."

He hung up. Raul had a big grin on his face. "Sounds like that little romance is budding out nicely."

"Budding?" Buck said. "I'd say it was in full bloom. But anticipating what information they are going to get I need for you to check the airlines and see if you can confirm her on a plane anywhere during that time period."

"I guess we should have already done that."

"We thought she had an alibi. There was no need."

"Okay, let's get on it. There's probably a high dollar lawyer wearing out horses coming here to make our life more difficult."

◊

"It seems like every time I ask you where you want to go to eat it ends up being Mexican food, usually the same place."

Helen laughed. "It does, doesn't it? I do love it. Jiggs used to say the same thing." The smile faded. "Oh dear," she put her hand over her mouth momentarily before going on. "I have to quit doing that."

"Doing what?"

"Bringing up Jiggs. It's not fair to you."

"I thought we had that settled. I don't mind. I accept that we are a threesome. It'll lessen over time and in the meantime I understand."

He reached across and took her hand.

"You are very understanding."

"It's something I tell young couples in counseling all the time. Fights happen in new relationships because people are being selfish. When both of them are thinking all the time about what's best for the other person instead of worrying about their own needs, those needs get met better than they can imagine. You can always count on me to put your needs first."

"I believe that, and you can count on me to do the same." She gave him a very direct look. "It sounds like we are making some pretty long term plans?"

"I came prepared to make some long-term plans."

Buck got out of his chair and got down on one knee. He pulled a blue velvet box from his pocket and opened it. The good size diamond on the ring caught the light and sparkled. The restaurant got quiet. Everyone had noticed it. Service stopped, and even the waitresses stood watching.

"You seem to have everyone's attention," she said softly.

"Your attention is the only one that counts right now. Helen, I guess I have loved you for much of my life only I kept that love squashed down because you belonged to another man, a good man. But now I can let it out and my how it bloomed when I opened the lid on it. I seem to begrudge every minute I spend away from you. So you know what I'm getting around to, will you marry me?"

"Buck, I feel exactly the same way and yes I will marry you."

When he slipped the ring on her finger, and they stood to embrace, the restaurant erupted in cheers and applause. People came over to wish them well. Miguel himself came from the back with a cake in hand. "This was for an event tomorrow, but phoo, we will cut it now. I will bake them another. Cake and champagne for the house!"

"Thank you so much, my friend, but do you suppose you might have some of the non-alcoholic variety?"

"I have the sparkling cider, of course. Tell me, Buck, are you going to perform your own wedding?"

Buck laughed. "I don't know how to do that. I think I'll let my friend over at First Baptist do it instead."

CHAPTER 23

R aul leaned over and whispered conspiratorially, "His name is J. Herbert Fontague."

"Well la-ti-dah. I bet he's costing her a pretty penny. Do we have the information back from Floyd and Carol?"

"Yes, and here is the information from the airline."

"Okay, let's go get to it."

Raul shook his head. "First I believe congratulations are in order."

Buck broke out in a big grin. "Yes, they are."

They shook hands as Raul clasped a hand on his shoulder. "I couldn't be happier for you."

"That's fair enough because I couldn't be happier myself." They stood that way clasping hands for what seemed like a long time, Then Buck erased the grin from his face, composed himself and said, "Okay, let's go get 'em."

They went in and got seated. The lawyer in his thousand-dollar suit looked down his nose at the country peace officer in front of him and with disdain said, "To begin with, my client should have never talked to you without me present. Anything that she said will be challenged in court, and I assure you I will have it set aside."

Buck smiled. He loved for people to underestimate him, it gave him an edge they weren't expecting. "I don't think so. We read her rights to her and she chose not to have a lawyer. We have it on tape. And we have sufficient evidence to back it up every detail of her confession so it won't be a problem."

Buck played the interrogation tape for them. When he finished the lawyer said, "I'll get that thrown out of court."

"You can try. When we back it up with the hospital confirming that the surgery that was supposedly her alibi was a small outpatient procedure that left her plenty of time to get here and airline records that put her on a plane that got here in time and didn't return for two days, I think it'll stand."

The lawyer sighed. "It probably will."

"What are you saying?" Mrs. Sessions asked.

"I'm saying they pretty much have you cold, my dear. You would be better served with me trying to make you a good deal."

She looked like a balloon that was deflating. "I thought—"

"You thought what all clients think, that I would magically get you off on a technicality. But it appears our good Sheriff has dotted his I's and crossed his T's." He fastened an appraising look on Buck who managed to look composed and noncommittal. "But I suspect his case against his primary suspect is not as solid."

Buck shook his head. "Oh, we have him solid as well." He waited a couple of moments for impact, "But I wouldn't object to it being stronger."

"Perhaps we could talk about a reduced sentence if she would testify? Maybe see if we could get her into an institution more befitting her station in life?"

"I have already put that exact offer on the table."

"Then I am not sure why I am here." He turned to her. "The Sheriff is making you an excellent offer. I recommend you take it.

I shall represent you at trial, but in my opinion, this is the best you are going to do. You are free of course to get another attorney and let them try."

"There is apparently no use."

"I would say not."

The lawyer left and Buck had Mrs. Sessions returned to lock-up. This time in his own jail.

"Doesn't matter if they talk together now. Make arrangement for transfer out to the women's facility at the prison awaiting trial. I wish I did have time to listen in, I suspect Brown is going to have some choice words for her."

"Will do."

"And while you are at it have Sessions and Mrs. Brown get back over here."

"I'm on it."

◊

They were waiting on him. The porch was overflowing with every chair taken but his rocker. There were even people sitting on the porch railing. They all stood and applauded as he got out of the car.

As he stepped up on the porch, he said, "Barney, I don't know why you bother putting out that newspaper, the grapevine is so much faster and far more effective."

"That very thing has occurred to me many times, Buck. I suppose my role is just to confirm what people already know. But let me be the first to congratulate you." He looked around. "Well, at least the first on the porch to do so.

Several minutes was spent in hand-shaking and individual congratulations. Buck got a cold drink and sat in the seat of honor.

Doc said, "When's the wedding?"

"Helen said she's had her big wedding. We are going to have a small private affair at her house with Donaldson from the First Baptist officiating."

"You mean we don't get to come?"

"Of course, you get to come, it won't be *that* small."

"I for one wouldn't miss it, invited or not." Doc pronounced. "But let's talk about the really big item. What is to become of the porch group? I know Helen is not going to want to leave the ranch."

"It's true I am already quite comfortable with the ranch as much time as I have spent there, but I promised the porch group would continue uninterrupted and it will."

"So out with it, how are you going to do that? You going to keep the house just for that purpose?"

"Actually, I would if that is what it took, but I have something else in mind. More than one option actually, but I need to confirm a few things before I can say which option I'm going to do. Just trust me that no matter which option works out the group will remain and I will continue to come. Who knows? Maybe not by myself."

◊

Buck didn't mind trials, in fact, he rather enjoyed them. At this point, he could sit back and watch as the prosecutor took his evidence and made the case. He would be called to testify, of

174

course, but he was comfortable with the facts, comfortable getting up in front of a group, and didn't mind doing it.

The judge called it to order and listened to opening statements. The parties had agreed to both cases in a single trial since two trials would be a duplicate of each other. The lawyer suggested that such a duplication would tend to annoy both the court and the jury and might even work to their disadvantage. Buck figured it had more to do with the man not wanting to spend any more time in this little town than necessary.

Buck had to admit that Fontague cut a very imposing figure, polished and confident. He objected when facts against his client were introduced into evidence, but the judge sustained none of them.

The attorney for Brown was a local and obviously awed by the big city lawyer. He too tried to object to evidence being introduced but with similar results. With the evidence in place, it fell to Buck to put a 'face' on it. He was called to the stand and sworn in.

"State your name please."

"Sheriff Buck Green."

"How long have you held that position?"

"Twenty-two years."

"You were the first person on the scene when the body was discovered?"

"Clem and Billy Bob over there were first. I was the first law enforcement officer on the scene."

"We'll get to their statements. What did you find when you arrived?"

Buck laid it out. He explained how Little Bear had deciphered the tracks and how the things he had predicted had proven to be completely accurate. He described the method of death and why they had focused their search for the killer on a man and a woman.

He walked them through the investigation, detailed their various actions in Houston and what those contacts had yielded. He was even forthcoming about the dead ends they had found and subsequently had to abandon. He carefully laid brick on brick, guided by the questions of the prosecutor until the evidence had built a wall around the pair. A wall of facts.

Facing this wall of facts, Mrs. Sessions was called to the stand. She was sworn in and took a seat.

"Mrs. Sessions, please allow me to set the scene by playing this tape of your interrogation." He played it. When it finished, he said, "Mrs. Sessions can you affirm that this tape has not been altered in any manner?"

She looked at her attorney and he nodded so she said, "It has not."

Let us go on to the second tape where you had an attorney present. That tape was played and again she was asked to confirm that it was accurate. Again her attorney nodded, and she did so.

"Mrs. Sessions, for the jury will you stipulate that you have agreed to turn states evidence in exchange for a reduced sentence as the tape indicates."

"I have."

"Will you in your own words tell us what you know of the events in chronological order?"

"You stupid broad," Brown yelled. "If you do this I'll get you for it."

The judge banged his gavel. "You will be silent, Mr. Brown or I will have you removed from the court."

The prosecutor moved closer to her and smiled. "Don't let him intimidate you, Mrs. Sessions. He's a three-time loser. When he goes in, he won't be coming back out. He won't be getting anyone. The outcome of this trial doesn't even entirely depend on your testimony, but in order for the state to stand good on their offer, you need to be forthcoming."

The witness had paled considerably. She cleared her throat and said. "I suspected my husband was cheating on me. I hired a private investigator to prove it, and he did. My original intention was to use it as grounds for a divorce. You see, I'm quite wealthy, and I wanted sufficient grounds so he could lay no claim to our assets whatsoever. I should have stayed with that plan."

She was twisting a handkerchief in her hands. This was obviously hard for her. "I did have a small medical procedure, but it was outpatient, and I immediately got on a plane to meet with the investigator. I already knew what he had found out, but I wanted him to arrange for me to see the woman involved. I suppose I'm vain enough that I wanted to see what she looked like, see what my husband seemed to prefer her over me."

She sniffed and blew her nose daintily into her handkerchief. "I knew who the woman's husband was as well so I made contact. In retrospect, I wish I had never done it. He wanted to be in on the meeting. He was, how shall I say it? A very unsettling influence. He got me quite worked up, and I suppose I lost it. The next thing I knew I had arranged for Brown to kill my husband so I could be sure he would not get any of my money."

She seemed on the verge of breaking down but visibly composed herself. "We drove outside of town to talk to the investigator where we would not be seen together. We had no intention of doing anything to Mr. Abernathy, at least I didn't think so. I was shocked and stunned when Brown got into an argument with him and more so when he pulled out a tire iron and hit the man."

She looked over at Brown who was muttering under his breath. "I saw what a dangerous man I had aligned myself with. I then knew that he fully intended to kill both his wife and my husband and would not hesitate to kill me as well if I became a problem. I was trapped by my own ignorance. I allowed a moment of anger toward my husband to escalate into a life-changing event. I felt I was the victim, and I was." She bowed her head and looked down. "But as the Sheriff pointed out, my response was very inappropriate."

On cross-examination, her attorney worked hard to make her as sympathetic as possible. The verdict was inevitable. He was now working on getting the sentence reduced as much as possible.

Brown took the stand and was sworn. He was surly, and it was clear he would be uncooperative. He was sewn up tight, and he knew it.

The prosecutor advanced on him. "Mr. Brown, you have pleaded not guilty."

"That's right. This is a frame, no matter what that uppity broad says."

"You maintain that you did not kill Delbert Abernathy?"

"I did not. She's just making this stuff up so she can get

herself a deal."

"If she is making it up, that would mean she did not solicit you to murder her husband, and that is all she is charged with."

He gave her an evil grin. "No, she solicited me all right, but I never agreed to do it. She's guilty right enough."

"But you maintain she is lying about you killing Abernathy?"

"Of course, she's lying, what else could she do? I went out there with them all right. I even had words with the guy. But while we was jawing at each other she slipped up behind him and hit him with a tire iron. She's lying because she's the one that killed him, not me."

What? I didn't see this coming, Buck thought. *Is this possible? Have I fallen for the sob story that woman gave me? Maybe I do tend to be too trusting. Maybe the preacher is winning out.*

"On the wiretap, Mrs. Sessions asked if the job was done."

"Sure she did, she wanted to know if I had killed her husband. I never said I would, though. This whole thing is her trying to lay it off on me, and everybody is eager to believe it because of my record. It's her word against mine, and mine doesn't count for much. She's really smooth, she is."

He laughed. "You, that judge, even that country bumpkin Sheriff, all taken in by a pretty face. What a laugh."

"Your honor," the prosecutor said. "In light of this new counter-accusation may we have a recess to confer on it?"

The prosecutor went with Buck down to his office. When they sat down, he said, "I have to tell you that was very convincing. It has me wondering if we have the right person charged."

"It had me wondering the same thing."

CHAPTER 24

They sat there thinking for a bit before Buck said, "Bottom line, we have to prove it was him and not her that hit Abernathy."

"Exactly," the prosecutor said.

"I've been thinking back to the scene, and the whole thing hinges on Little Bear's interpretation of the tracks."

"Which is not exactly a science."

Buck smiled. "I think it may be more concrete than you think."

He picked up the phone and called Little Bear, quickly briefed him and told him to get down there before the recess ended. Then he hollered at Carol and told her to get her video of the crime scene ready to show again.

By the time the judge gaveled the trial back into session, Little Bear was in the back of the room.

The prosecutor stood and called him to the stand. He came forward and was sworn in.

"Please state your name."

"Charley Little Bear."

"You are an Indian?"

"I am a full-blood Navajo."

The prosecutor was pacing in front of him as he asked the questions. "And what is your profession?"

"I am a part-time deputy for the Sheriff's department. I am

also a professional hunter, guide, and tracker."

The prosecutor halted in front of him and leaned in close. "Surely tracking has gone the way of gunfights and Wyatt Earp and the OK Corral. It is bound to be outdated and no longer used."

"It is useless in the big cities where all the surfaces are paved. But in small communities like ours where there is unpaved ground and unpaved roads, it is as effective as it ever has been. Any time there is a surface that will hold a track, animals and automobiles and men still make them."

"You say tracking is still effective, how effective would that be?"

"I have brought a file with me with letters of commendation from a number of law enforcement people who testify how my tracking skills were instrumental in capturing suspects or making cases against them."

"Judge, allow me to place this file in evidence as Exhibit F."

"So noted."

The prosecutor turned back to Little Bear. "You have been briefed on the counter-accusation the defendant, in this case, has made?"

"I have."

"Do you have an opinion on it?"

"It is a lie."

Brown erupted again with some choice words about Little Bear's heritage and whether or not his mother actually knew who his father was. In short some very creative profanity.

The big Navajo's face was devoid of emotion, stoic.

"Can you prove it is a lie?"

"I can."

They set up a big screen to project on. "We are going to return to the footage Deputy Tatum took at the scene. We saw portions of it earlier but this time, we are going to the section where Deputy Little Bear analyzes the tracks. I might add that the facts have borne out everything he said about them."

As the video ran Little Bear's voice was clear narrating his findings. He went along with the narration pointing with a pointer to the things he was commenting on. He showed how he established who the tracks belonged to their size and weight. He showed how he had ruled out those who were at the scene. He pointed out the tracks of the two suspects on trial now although he indicated they did not know who those tracks belonged to at the time.

Then he had the image frozen. "Sometimes it is not the tracks that are there that tell the story, but what is not there."

He moved over to the other side of the screen and pointed. "You see here the tracks of Abernathy, and here the tracks of Brown confronting him as he has admitted. Here are the tracks of Mrs. Sessions stopping at the front of the car."

"What is missing?" He looked over at Brown. "You can clearly see there are no tracks coming up behind Abernathy."

The prosecutor rested his case, and the defense had no cross-examination. Brown was toast. The judge remanded the case to the jury.

◊

Buck walked from the second floor of the courthouse back

down to his office to find Steve Sessions and Susan Brown waiting on him. His secretary had already seated them in the chairs across from his desk. He came in, left his hat on the hat rack and took a seat.

"I'm guessing you two feel a bit relieved."

Susan smiled and looked up. "You have no idea, Sheriff. For so many years I've been living under the threat of constant abuse. You just can't understand the weight that has been lifted from me."

"No, I suppose I can't."

Steve reached out to take her hand and smile at her. Then turned his attention to Buck. "My marriage was miserable for years, but I don't believe in divorce. I really fought it. I know you are a part-time minister, I know you don't approve of the affair we had."

"Not for me to judge people, that's the Lord's business. But as a person, you're right, I don't approve." He let those words sink in for a moment. "But the Lord also said if you would return to him he would return to you. He is faithful to forgive."

"Adultery is a big fence to climb over."

"Don't you get it? To God sin is sin. From murder to a little white lie, God hates sin. That's why the only way he could redeem us from that sin was to send his own son to redeem us with a blood sacrifice. He also knows we are imperfect creatures who will continue to be sinners no matter how hard we try. The only difference for us is we are sinners who have been forgiven."

"What are you saying?"

"I'm saying you two need to get down on your knees together and take your sins to the Lord. And you need to get into reading his word…a lot. He'll show you the way forward, and he *will* forgive you if you get right with him. Am I right that you two are going to be staying together?"

They smiled at each other. "Oh yes."

"Then do it right. File the papers and get free of those partners. Steve, if you don't, she's going to do it anyway. And Susan, you might as well, your husband isn't coming back. There's no reason you two can't take it from here and make yourselves a good life."

"God forgiving us doesn't mean we can forgive ourselves, preacher...I mean Sheriff."

"I reckon right now I do have my preacher hat on…or off as it were. That's a common malady for Christians, Steve. But we don't realize what we are saying if we say that. Saying we can't forgive ourselves means that our own forgiveness is more important than the forgiveness of the Lord. You don't mean to say that do you?"

"Of course not."

"Then when the Lord forgives he puts it away and completely forgets it. We need to do the same. Living in the past just steals joy from the future. You need to go and ask that forgiveness, look to the Bible to hear him speak to you, and it wouldn't hurt you to get back in church. I have one I can recommend if you like."

"We had already talked about coming to your church if you would have us. I can work from the office here as easy as anywhere, and I don't really have much in Houston to go back to."

"Happy to have you. We're all just a bunch of forgiven sinners trying to live the best we can."

"We were both more active in church than we are now. Over

the years it has gotten easier and easier for both of us to miss."

"The Bible warns us against forsaking gathering with fellow believers. That's an important part of our faith staying strong, and you're right, it does get easier and easier. But one important tool for that is being equally yoked with another believer where we can strengthen each other to attend. When one of you is looking to take any excuse to miss the other is there to prop up their resolve."

Raul stuck his head in. "Buck, the jury is coming back."

Buck looked at the couple. "Let's go listen to them telling you your life can start over."

They filed up to the second floor. They took a seat just as the judge said, "Have you reached a verdict?"

The foreman indicated that they had, and the paper was passed to the judge. He read it and said, "So say you all?"

They nodded in unison so he asked the defendants to stand.

He looked at Brown and said, "God has smiled on you today, Ken Brown, the jury has found you guilty but has passed over the death sentence and given you life without parole."

"Life behind bars, I ain't sure they done me any favors."

"Perhaps not but that's what you are looking at." He turned his attention to Alice Sessions. "Mrs. Sessions, had you been implicated in the death of Abernathy you would have been facing the same sentence as an accomplice. But the trial showed you had no involvement in that other than being an unwilling witness. But you have been found guilty on conspiracy to commit murder. It is a felony and carries a penalty from twenty years to life."

Her knees seemed to fail her, and her attorney had to support her to keep her from going down. The judge went on. "However, under the plea deal your attorney negotiated, and because the jury found you sympathetic and contrite, the jury has reduced it to ten years, place of incarceration to be determined."

"It could be worse." She said quietly

"Are you kidding?" her attorney said. "That's very good. If you are a model prisoner you could win parole in five or six years."

"Five or six years sounds like a lifetime."

"So how would twenty to life have sounded?"

"Like a death sentence."

◊

"Ah," Buck said, "Just the people I was wanting to see."

Floyd and Carol came in the door. Buck could see a rental truck out in the parking lot.

"We just came by for a minute. We have to go find him a place to live."

"Come sit down for a minute first. Did you hear about the trial?"

"We've been a little busy," Carol said.

"Brown just got a life sentence and Alice Sessions got her sentence reduced to ten years."

Floyd smiled. "So it's finally over."

"You were a big part of it, and we appreciate it," Buck said.

"I enjoyed it."

He looked at Carol. "I don't mean to be nosy, but is that a ring on your finger?"

She laughed, "It sure is. We're engaged."

"I was fully expecting that, and in light of that I have a proposition for you."

"A proposition."

"I'm going to be moving out of my house. It's a nice little house, and I would only allow it to go into the right hands. It does have to be the 'right' hands because any rental or lease purchase arrangement will have a condition attached to it."

Floyd was surprised. "Are you offering us your house?"

"That depends on whether you agree to the condition or not."

"What is it?"

"I promised the porch group they would always have a place to gather, and I meant it even if I have to keep the house just for that purpose."

Floyd didn't understand. "What's a porch group?"

"Oh, you'll love it," Carol said, "I know I do. It's a bunch of delightful gentlemen who gather each day to hash over what's going on in town. If you're lucky enough to be in the porch group you are in the know about everything. I don't know about you, but I would love to live in the house where the porch group meets."

"If you love it I'll love it. What will the rent be?"

"Well, I know how much you make so it won't put a strain on you. And you can do lease-purchase if you want. We'll make it fit whatever you need it to be. But there is one more condition."

"Name it."

"My rocking chair stays, and I expect to use it…a lot."

Carol folded her arms. "Actually, we have one more condition too."

"And that would be what?

"You officiate our wedding."

"Done. Although I was kind of hoping to walk you down the aisle."

"Can't you do both?"

"Hadn't thought about that. I might could figure something out. I can see it now. I'd walk you down all proud and proper. Then I'd jump on the other side and say, "Who gives this woman?" Then I'd jump back and say "I do." Then I'd hand you over to him and jump back again. That could work."

They both laughed. "I could just see that," Floyd said.

"Then we have a deal?"

All three joined hands, "Deal."

◊

Buck told Helen about his plans and she fully approved. One point she wasn't sure about, though. "Buck, I am so happy I get to continue to live here. Are you sure you won't be uncomfortable about it? The threesome, you know?"

"Not at all."

"You know you would be better qualified to run the ranch than Jimmy."

"Nice of you to say, but that's not true. He has trained for years to do it, and he is perfectly suited for it. No, if you have no objection I have no intention of giving up either the badge or the Bible. It's true I may get too old to effectively tote the badge at some point, but if you want to know when I plan on retiring from preaching? I plan to do it the day after Satan announced that HE is retiring."

"I'm glad you aren't quitting. It'd be hard for me to think of you any other way."

The next two days went by in a blur, getting the house ready, the kids coming in, making all the plans. The morning before the service Buck sat down with the kids to make sure they were on the same page.

"I've known all of you since you were born. You've always been like you were my kids too. But I have to tell you, you aren't. I'll never try to replace your father, and I'll never do anything that might reflect badly on his memory. You know me, I loved the man too. But I'll be here for you any way that I can. The most important thing to remember is the fact that I plan to do anything and everything to make your mother happy."

He looked around at their faces. Nobody seemed to be objecting. "I loved both of them, but now that love toward her has deepened into something else. I never would have allowed it to do that while Jiggs was alive but maybe your mother knew that she had two men in love with her. I'm sorry it took the passing of Jiggs for it to happen, but I am happy that I can finally express that love."

They looked at each other. With unspoken consent, Linda was elected spokesman. "Most of our life you were Uncle Buck to us, and we do know how much you loved them and yes we knew it was both of them. It says a lot about you that you kept your own feelings in check all of these years. Just so you know we don't have any reservations about you marrying mother, none at all because we know you will make her happy. She has told us that you are going to live on the ranch with her, and we're happy about that too. We really can't see her living anywhere else. If it is what you are looking for, you have our unconditional blessing."

CHAPTER 25

Her second son Harold walked Helen down the stairs headed to the big fireplace where Buck and the preacher stood waiting. She was dressed simply in a powder blue dress and Buck had gone all out and bought a new suit.

He saw her coming down the stairs and thought, *If I still had any lingering doubts as to whether I was doing the right thing or not they are gone now. I have to be the luckiest man alive. Thirty years ago I knew she was my soulmate but fate intervened, and I've had that fire tamped down all these years. But God in his wisdom has decided to give me a second chance.*

The room was overflowing with friends and among others included the full complement of the porch group and much of Buck's congregation. Helen started getting an inkling of how her life was going to change being a pastor's wife.

She arrived at the fireplace, and Harold stood between them. Brother Donaldson looked at them and said, "Who gives this woman?"

Harold said, "My father in absentia and her four children."

Donaldson cocked an eyebrow at that one, but the ones who needed to understand got it. Harold took his mother's hand, placed it in Bucks' hand and backed out to go find a seat.

"These days so many couples simply want to say their own vows and Buck and Helen have chosen to do the same."

He looked at Helen and said, "Ladies first."

Buck took both of her hands in his own. They locked eyes, and she started. "For you and for all of our friends who have gathered here and may need to hear the whole story. For almost as far back as I can remember anytime I have needed you, you have been there, strong and dependable. Harold said his father and the children were giving me to you. Many here may not understand that but the two of us as well as the children believe Jiggs is still with us, and we believe he approves of this union very much."

A single tear slid slowly down her cheek. "I have always loved you as much as I did him. And I know you loved him as much as you do me. It was a strange bond, but a good one. And now, through Harold, he has given me to you. Our love has matured to a different level, but I pledge myself to you, now and forever."

Buck's turn, but the man who could preach on Sundays and give political talks and public relations talks during the week suddenly found a lump in his throat and difficulty speaking. "I have always thought you were my soulmate and it has been hard taking a back seat to another man, even my best friend. But it was a love I would have never acted on nor would you. But the Lord has chosen to give us our time, and I will be eternally grateful."

He cleared his throat trying to keep his voice going a little longer. "Helen, the love I had to share for so long is now yours alone, and it is deeper and wider and longer than ever. I pledge you my love, my protection, my companionship, my understanding for as long as I may live. Then I will carry it forward into eternity where it will be the three of us again but where love is so unbounded that what we have will have it without measure."

They exchanged rings, then Donaldson pronounced them man and wife. Buck gave her something of a shy kiss which earned him catcalls from all his friends.

◊

During the meet and greet Raul came up to congratulate him, and Buck said, "Thanks. Who's watching the store?"

"Best be hoping things continue to stay peaceful, we're running a skeleton crew. Those that aren't here are over at your house moving your stuff out and Floyd and Carol's stuff in."

"Make sure they know that all the appliances and any furniture that they want they are welcome to it."

"They said you told them that."

"Any that they don't want you can take to the Salvation Army."

"I'll make sure they know that."

"And make sure they know the fridge stays on the porch."

"They know, Buck, they understand the conditions. We've got this, and they are looking forward to the porch group. But on to more important things, where are you going on your honeymoon?"

"We've got reservations right on the Riverwalk in San Antonio."

"That'll be nice."

"Yes, I expect it will be. I'm looking forward to it."

◊

Helen and Buck strolled hand in hand down the Riverwalk. They took one of the colorful river barges to get a water view of the sites along each bank. Brightly colored umbrellas were spread along much of the bank with places for outdoor dining. At night there were lights strung everywhere and it was lit up to be a magical place.

The first day Helen could hardly wait to take the short trip over to see the Alamo and spend hours immersed in the history of the beginning of her beloved state. As always she understood traveling for Buck meant finding great places to eat and he understood Helen's love for Mexican food always had to be factored in. That was just fine with him as was quite fond of it himself. With its rich Mexican heritage, there were a lot of them to choose from including Casa Rio, the first restaurant on the Riverwalk back in 1946. The food was wonderful.

They took the mission tour to see the Spanish Missions, in addition to the Alamo, spread around the area and saw the famous Rose Window. They went through the San Antonio Botanical Garden which was breathtaking. They passed on the strenuous activity of Six Flags but did find a variety of entertainment available. Helen particularly loved the Mariachi Bands and the dancers with their bright Spanish skirts.

They strolled through endless shops and Buck discovered she loved to go shopping, but that didn't mean she did a lot of buying. Mostly she liked to look. By the second day, his boots remained in the hotel room in favor of some new tennis shoes. Helen discovered the attractively stitched Guayabera shirts which were worn outside the pants rather than tucked in. These shirts in that culture were also called 'wedding shirts' and were considered quite dressy. She bought Buck several and to his surprise he found them very comfortable and liked them a lot. That's what he wore the remainder of the week.

They took the elevator up to the top of the Tower of the Americas where they ate seafood in a restaurant that slowly turned as they dined spreading out the lights of the city for them to see. But the thing they loved the most was just the time together. They seemed to love the same things, have the same dislikes and Buck couldn't help but think he had finally found the other half of himself that at long last had made him whole.

◊

A week later Buck and Helen drove up to his old house. He was actually a bit surprised that the porch group was in place. They walked across the lawn and as they stepped up on the porch the first thing they noticed was not only Buck's rocker sitting there empty, but an identical matching rocker sitting next to it. Both had big red bows on them.

"I don't know what to say, guys. I'm really moved."

"Well, don't get sloppy sentimental on us," Barney said.

"Yeah," Doc added. "We got enough of that at the wedding."

Buck got two cold drinks and brought one to Helen who was already sitting in her rocker. "Just so you know, those chairs will be empty if you aren't in them."

Carol came out of the house, "Buck! Helen! You're back! Here, take one, these just came out of the oven."

She offered them a plate of hot chocolate chip cookies, then started offering them around. "I guess you might notice there has been something of an upgrade around here," Doc said. "Carol is the ultimate porch group hostess."

Buck marveled at what he was seeing. "Every time I turn around I see a new side of you, Carol."

"Don't get the wrong idea, I don't do this every day. But I like to do it now and then. I figured today would be a good choice because we expected you back today."

"She's got all of us doing it, Buck," Barney said. "Would you believe I even baked a chocolate cake the other day?"

"And I brought in some donuts," Doc said. "I don't bake. I barely cook. Actually, I have a freezer full of TV dinners."

"You poor baby," Helen said. "We'll have to have you over and feed you some real food."

"Let it be known that I have no problem accepting a sympathy meal if you are the one cooking it, Helen."

"Well, I have to say I am surprised by all this."

"Admit it, Buck," Little Bear said. "You really thought this group would fall apart if you weren't here to hold it together."

"Maybe I did. Does that mean I've got a big ego? Or maybe an inflated sense of self-importance?"

"It's more like you are a proud parent who is afraid to let go of their children's hand and let them walk on their own."

"I have a little trouble seeing you guys as my children, Barney."

"It's a metaphor, Buck, or is it a simile? You'd think a newspaper man would know the difference."

"I'm going with simile, and I do get it."

Carol squatted by Buck's chair and put a hand on his arm. When you get settled back in and unpacked, we've got a wedding to plan."

Buck smiled at her, "We do indeed."

"We'd like to have it at your church. And we'd like it to be soon, I'm anxious to move in here with him."

Helen got out of her chair and helped Carol up. "Let's go inside and talk about it, dear. Buck just says the words, we ladies have to do the planning."

ABOUT THE AUTHOR

Terry is a former literary agent and an author with over 40 books in print, a number of articles, short stories, internet content and a variety of other writing credits as well as an educator and consultant with a reputation for  presenting to conferences all over the country. He says he grew up watching *Gunsmoke* and Bonanza on TV and watching Gene and Roy in Saturday morning matinees. He has a love for the western genre and as a deeply religious man; his faith is often evident in his books whether he is intentionally writing it in or not. A bookstore of his available works, as well as a periodic blog, can be found his website: www.terryburns.net and on Amazon at http://bit.ly/Terrys-Bookstore

Some of his books currently available in print include:

The Badge and the Bible – Contemporary Christian Western. A small-town Sheriff must learn to walk the line between the badge and the Bible.

The Badge and the Bride – Contemporary Christian Western. The Sheriff is a confirmed bachelor, but when he investigates a murder, he may find more than a killer.

Hounded – Traditional Christian Western. A young man is falsely convicted of murdering his mother, and the only way he can clear himself is to escape and find the real killer.

Saint's Roost – Historical Christian Romance. A young woman finds herself alone on the open prairie, where she discovers courage and determination she did not know she had ...and in the process, love.

Beyond the Smoke – Christian Young Adult that won the Will Rogers Medallion. A young man is left alone after a wagon train is destroyed. He has to grow up fast – or not grow up at all.

The Mysterious Ways Series – Traditional Christian Westerns.

Mysterious Ways – A con-man hides in the guise of a preacher to get away with his scams, only to find himself having to fill the role for real.

Brother's Keeper – Two identical twins take different paths in life –one good and the other the outlaw trail – but their paths intersect.

Shepherd's Son – The death of his father forces a young man to do the only thing he can to save the ranch, bring sheep into cattle country – with violent results.

Second Chances – A grandfather dying of cancer puts a detective on the trail of his estranged son. Will he be found in time for second chances?

Hard Choices – Historical Fiction – A young mountain boy accidentally kills another but the family declares a blood feud and chases him all over Texas.

Don't I Know You? – What would life be like if everyone you met thought they knew you? Larry Smith finds this is not always a good thing.

Stone Age Cowboy – An orphan grew up by becoming a bull-rider, but when he is kicked in the head by a bull, he goes into a coma with totally unexpected results.

Trails of the Dime Novel – A naïve young man goes west to write the delicious little novels that were so popular in the day – and to share the adventures that went with them.

On the Road Home-Stories of Love and Life – A collection of Terry's short stories and poetry.

Writing in Obedience – With editorial assistant Linda Yezak – A nonfiction writing primer for Christian writers.

Sample chapter from *Saint's Roost* by Terry Burns:

CHAPTER 1

1879 Santa Fe Trail

A wagon leaving the safety of a wagon train to strike out by itself is a lonesome sight.

Its occupants, Patrick and Janie Benedict were headed west in an old Conestoga that complained at every bump and jolt in the road. The wheels squealed a high-pitched, irritating sound. Still, it was marginally dependable. More dependable were the four Missouri mules that drew it, depending on their mood and disposition at the moment.

The young couple looked the part, him tall and handsome with the sincere brown eyes appropriate for a young minister. The prairie heat made shirtsleeves mandatory and he peered out from under a flat-brimmed black hat indicative of those who pursued the avocation of a circuit-riding preacher.

His bride of only a year sat next to him, simply clad in a checked dress and plain white bonnet. Her hair peeked out from the bonnet and lit up scarlet red when the sun touched it. Both their faces were brighter from barely contained excitement and enthusiasm than from the rays of the hot summer sun.

They made the trek west because Patrick had been called to the ministry. More specifically, he had felt himself called to do missionary work in what he referred to as the wild, wild West. Not that he had to go so far to find sinners; there was certainly more sin right there in certain sections of St. Louis than would be found in the entire west.

Yet many of his seminary classmates knew that in the secret compartments of his mind, Patrick saw himself in a saintly pose, surrounded by a throng of half-naked savages kneeling about him as he converted them in droves by the power of his magnificent oratory. Such ambitious visions were certainly encouraged at the seminary.

Still, some of his teachers thought him very naive. Others thought him to be headstrong while the more optimistic conceded he had a *unique evangelistic drive*. The term the wagon master came up with when a couple of young people still in their twenties left the train alone was...well...to be truthful...stupid.

◊

Quite a distance back up the wagon trail, pint-size Ruben Dunn had his own ideas. He had these ideas on virtually any subject you could name, and he didn't mind sharing them with anyone inclined to listen.

Ruben's alter ego and long-time saddle mate was a tall drink of water by the name of Frank Walker. Had Frank ever been caught asleep at the wrong place, someone might have mistakenly used him to try to repair a length of split rail fence. Frank had dark hair that defied any comb in existence, chocolate brown eyes, and was unfailingly good humored and easy going.

More important, and absolutely essential to have a friendship with Ruben, he knew his own mind and did not feel it necessary to debate various points with his confident, but diminutive companion. Once Frank made up his mind, he simply went ahead and did what he wanted without much, if any, discussion.

Ruben on the other hand could debate the finer points of doing something different the entire time he calmly followed Frank's lead. The fact that he espoused one course of action while he did another never seemed to be a problem; it was merely how life worked. It certainly had nothing to do with diluting the opinions Ruben might hold.

At the present time, the pair drifted with no particular destination in mind. Ruben did have some thoughts on where they should go and what they should do, however. He tipped his hat back on his head to reveal a shock of blonde hair with the look and consistency of prairie straw. He squeezed off his ever-present grin to compress his face into a more thoughtful expression, closed both hands on top of his saddle horn and ventured his opinion.

"What I think," Ruben said, "is we could get us a ranch started down Texas way. There's loose stock, mavericks they call them, all over the place, and they're ours for the taking if we want to put up the hard work. There's land available that can be had mighty cheap. The land of opportunity, that's what they call it, and that's what it is. We could call our ranch the Dunn-it ranch. I can almost see the sign over the gate," he looked off into the distance as if he could see the very sight he was describing.

"You being the Dunn and me being the *it*, I suppose." No trace of emotion showed on Frank's face to indicate whether he might be kidding or not.

Ruben grimaced, "Aw, Frank, it ain't like that, it ain't like that at all, it's just a catchy name."

"If we branded cows with Dunn-it, they'd be barbequed while they was still on the hoof."

"Dang it, Frank, you got no imagination." Ruben let go of the saddle horn and poked the air vigorously in his partner's general direction to emphasize his point.

"That ain't so, and you know it. I ain't even hung up on a name, I just like to twist your tail a little ever' now and then. Keeps you humble." Frank may have had a hint of a smile on his face. With him it was hard to tell.

"I don't think it's possible to keep me humble, me being so nacherly great and all."

"On further thought, I kinda like the name. It'd make people feel sorry for me with what I have to put up with. You know, me being an 'it' would be plain enough for anybody." Ruben only looked at him as if unable to comprehend as he shook his head slowly side to side.

◊

"Janie," Patrick rested his hands on his knees, keeping gentle pressure on the reins. "I can hardly wait. I know I've been called to do great things. I tell you I'll convert so many of these heathens..."

Janie smiled, she had heard this day and night for a year, but she didn't mind. She was proud of the man she thought of as her young knight, and believed in his quest as strongly as he did. She had no doubt but what he would do exactly as he said he would do.

All the way down through Kansas he practiced his oratory, and he wrote sermons: moving, and powerful if flowery sermons.

His only congregation for these epistles, besides Janie, were the four Missouri mules. There was no record as to whether he converted them or not, as they were notoriously uncommunicative. The evidence certainly proved him to be a patient and pious man, however, as anyone who can drive a brace of such animals without the fortification of stout teamster cusswords, was a man of strong character, indeed.

Clearing the Kansas line took them into Indian Territory.

It was intentional. The wagon train had been primarily commercial and they felt out of place. The word going around was the railroad to Santa Fe was nearing completion and would soon replace the wagon trail entirely. Too much civilization, surely the unchurched Indians he searched for would be down in the territory.

Had they come straight down from St. Louis, it would have put them over in the country occupied by the Five Civilized Tribes. The tribes in that part of the territory were known for establishing farms and towns, and had centuries of beliefs and customs of their own which did not conflict strongly with Christian beliefs. It would have been fertile ground for Patrick's work.

But they didn't come directly south. They had consistently veered off to the right, and by the time they got through Kansas, they were well into the part of the territory known as no-man's land. It was a land inhabited by outlaws, and the Comanche and Kiowa, who roamed across the plains of Texas all the way up into western Kansas. Here, indeed, were exactly the inveterate sinners and naked savages Patrick had envisioned, and in quantities sufficient to fulfill any dream he may have had.

It was mid-morning when they met their first opportunity to

start his ministry. They topped a small rise in the sea of blowing grass they had been in for days. Suddenly, they saw ahead of them two magnificent mounted warriors on painted ponies.

They were tall, and naked to the sun except for a breechcloth and moccasins on their feet. Their faces were painted, and on their heads were feathered bonnets, which trailed well down their backs. They held shields with bright painted symbols on them in their left hands.

Patrick was elated. His first prospects. And exactly what he had envisioned in his dreams. He pulled the team up about 50 yards away, dismounted and tied them off to a ground hitch weight. The warriors watched curiously. He slipped into his black frock coat, picked up and clutched his Bible to his chest and started toward them with his hand held up in a sign of peace.

His smile was still fixed on his face when the arrow drove deep into his chest.

The great sermon he had practiced so long remained caught in his throat. His mind screamed, *No! I can't be denied my destiny. Janie, what will—*

Then he fell over on his face, and the last of his air gently left him as he went on to his reward.

CAST OF CHARACTERS

DELBERT ABERNATHY – Book 2: Houston Private Investigator and murder victim

MRS ABERNATHY – Book 2: Widow of slain Private Investigator - a slender woman with prematurely grey hair.

KEN BROWN – Book 2: abusive husband - jealous and has a terrible temper

SUSAN BROWN – Book 2: Wife of an abusive husband - was a brunette, middle-aged woman and looked to be in her late forties or early fifties – worked at Oilfield Supply

CLEM AND BILLY BOB – Book 2: Affable drunks who find a murder victim

LEE BOB COURTLAND – Book 1: Tennessee Mountain boy in jail for Moonshining takes a contract to perform a hit – later became a ranch hand on the Jorgenson ranch

RALPH DeGRASSI – Book 1: Mob boss

SANDY DENNIS – Book 1: Texas Department of Public Safety trooper

REV. DONALDSON: Pastor of First Baptist Church

MIKE DONOVAN Book 2: Local attorney representing Ferguson Supply

FLOYD DUCKWORTH – Book 2: Young rookie Harris County deputy

JACK DULANEY – Book 1: Hired hand at Junior Jorgenson's place was a splinter of a man, and he hefted a hay bale with as much difficulty as a person might expect of a man nearing seventy.

SHERIFF JERRY EVERLY – Book 2: Harris County Sheriff

CHIEF DEPUTY RAUL FERNANDEZ – Book 1 and 2: Stood six foot five without his boots on and weighed a rock solid 250 pounds. Years ago, when he filled out the job application to join the department, he hadn't classified himself as Hispanic, but instead noted that he had been born and raised in Clear Creek. That said a lot about how he thought of himself, but his features didn't leave his heritage in doubt whether he wrote it on the form or not.

JAMES FERGUSON – Book 2: Owner of Ferguson Supply

RUBEN GARCIA – Book 1: Jail escapee

MRS. FOLEY - Book 1 and 2: Owner of Dixie Lodge Motel

HERBERT J FONTAGUE – Book 2: Big-name Houston attorney

BUCK GREEN –Book 1 and 2: Small church pastor that had run for Sheriff a number of years back because he needed more income than the little church he pastored could provide. But he was well loved and everyone just naturally kept re-electing him. Even though Buck's men dressed in chocolate brown pants and khaki uniform shirts, he still wore the blue jeans and the striped western shirt of a rancher. It was only the gold badge on a leather flap hanging from his shirt pocket that identified him as a law enforcement officer.

BARNEY HOKE – Book 1 and 2: Regular porch gatherer. Barney didn't look much like a scrappy newspaper editor, more like an absent-minded professor. He wore a bow tie and one of his light-colored suits either in the oppressive heat of summer or in the dead of winter – didn't matter to him. His totally gray hair fell over his forehead almost to his dark-rimmed glasses.

BOB JENNINGS – Book 1: State Park Ranger

JUNIOR JORGENSON – Book 1: Local rancher who came up missing

CHARLEY LITTLE BEAR – Book 1 and 2: One of Buck's oldest friends. He was a full blood Navajo Indian. Little Bear wore his dark black hair caught up in two braids that fell below his shoulders, and his black, flat-brimmed hat sported a very colorful beaded hatband. He was even shorter than Buck, but significantly outweighed him. He was a world-class tracker and it was said he could track an ant across solid rocks.

DOC MALONE – Book 1 and 2: Doc had always reminded Buck of Milburn Stone, the actor that played the role of Doc on the TV show *Gunsmoke*, in looks, and in attitude. He smiled, he was pretty sure the comparison was something Doc did on purpose, right down to the hat always worn back on his head, the dark mustache, and the wire-rimmed glasses. Doc was an agnostic.

MIKE Book 1: Deputy
MIKE MILNER - Book 1: Manager of the Chamber of Commerce
JIM MINOR – Book 1: Houston garbage collection millionaire running against Buck for Sheriff
PENNY – Book 1 and 2: Dispatcher
CHUGG AND ZEKE ROGERS Book 1: brothers with long records who try to escape from custody.
SAM JACKSON – Book 2: Clear Creek Police Chief
DEBBYE SANCHEZ AND SONNORA McCALL Book 1: Teenagers who got involved with Jail escapee
JOHN SANDERS – Book 1: Hardheaded hardhat who takes Carol on in a fight
ALICE SESSIONS – Book 2: Hired Abernathy to investigate her husbands suspected affair - her hair was elaborately done; she was wearing an expensive looking pants suit. She looked more like she was on her way to the country club for lunch. She reeked of money.
STEVE SESSIONS – Book 2: Salesman for Oilfield Supply – cheating on his wife
HAROLD SILSBEE – BOOK 2: Husky, middle-aged man with dark, almost swarthy features.
HELEN SILSBEE –Book 2: Attractive lady, brunette, close to sixty years old but in spite of the expensive pant suit she had on, Buck knew she had been born and raised on a ranch and was pure cowgirl at heart.
JACK SILSBEE – Book 2: Harold and Jack both took after their dad, dark features that appeared even darker with the jet-black hair.
JIMMY SILSBEE – Book 2: The third brother and his sister Linda both took after their mother. They were light haired and easy going.
LINDA SILSBEE – Book 2 - Linda both took after their mother light haired and easy going.
JIGGS SILSBEE – Book 2: Rancher who passed away and one of Buck's closest friends
FLORENCE SIMMONS – Book 2: Secretary at Abernathy Investigations in Houston.

SUE – Book 1 and 2: Buck's secretary - a plus-sized woman with a round face and an ever-present smile.

CAROL TATUM - Book 1 and 2: Buck hired her she was fresh out of the Marines, hand-to-hand combat instructor with a black belt, and still in uniform. Her dishwater blonde hair crowded her face, but she was calm and disciplined an ex-marine to the core. The few times he had seen her out of uniform she had been in workout clothes or jeans. He realized he had never seen her nicely dressed. She had on a simple dress and had her hair down instead of pulled up under her hat. Her legs were sculpted and tanned. It just hadn't occurred to him that she was a beautiful young woman, but he realized it now.

CHARLEY THOMAS – Book 1: Wrecker operator

ANTONNIO "Tony" TORRELLI – Book 1: Hit man

WAYNE TUNNELL – Book 1 and 2: Buck's nephew.

ROGER WALKER – Book 2: Wife-abuser and employee at Ferguson Supply

DAVE WALOVICH – Book 1: Weasel of a hotel bellman

www.ingramcontent.com/pod-product-compliance
Lightning Source LLC
Chambersburg PA
CBHW060146130626
46556CB00006B/2518